ABSOLOM'S WAKE

by Nancy A. Collins

The one-eyed headman stepped forward while the others pinned the cooper's arms to his sides, keeping him from rolling free, and bared his horrible filed teeth. The cannibal's mouth seemed to grow to hideous proportions, like a snake unhinging its jaw, before he bit deep into Santo's exposed belly. The cooper's angry shouts quickly dissolved into shrieking, the likes of which I had never heard from a human being.

As I lay there in the shadows, paralyzed with horror, the one-eyed cannibal yanked free a length of my friend's guts, causing them to unravel from his torso like a magician's scarf. The savage then swallowed the mouthful of pulsing, living flesh whole, without the use of his hands, his throat seeming to expand as he gulped down his hideous meal. Excited by the smell of their victim's blood and the sight of his agonized thrashing, the remaining cannibals set upon poor, doomed Santo, ripping into his struggling body like a pair of boars rooting for truffles.

"Get off my porch, you bloody bastards!" His Lordship yelled as he charged out of the bungalow, armed with a native paddle-spear fashioned of koa wood. The Englishman attempted to brain the one-eyed cannibal with the oar blade, but his opponent proved far too swift. The savage dodged the blow while sweeping the aristocrat's legs out from under him, causing His Lordship to drop the weapon.

The cannibal headman then snatched up the paddle-spear and drove its business-end through His Lordship's chest, pinning him like a butterfly.

The sight of the blood spurting from the dying man's mouth, like the crimson geyser in my nightmare, shocked me from my paralysis. Leaping to my feet, I ran towards the beach and the direction of the *Absolom*. As I sped across the sandy beach, I heard angry shouts behind me. I glanced over my shoulder and instantly wished I had not looked. The trio of cannibals were in close pursuit, their tattooed faces smeared with the blood of my friends, their horrible, shark-like maws opened impossibly wide, as if to swallow me whole.

PART ONE

Gone A' Whaling

Chapter One

A Proper Introduction—My Uncle Calvin—The Dolphin Amulet—My Bequest

The story I am about to relate to you is a true and accurate account of the fate that befell the crew of the good ship *Absolom*, a whaler out of Sag Harbor, in the Year of Our Lord 1846. But before I begin my tale of amazement and woe, allow me to properly introduce myself.

My name is Jonah Padgett. I realize my Christian name is an unfortunate one, given my profession, for sailors are a superstitious breed, prone to seeing mermaids and sea serpents at the slightest provocation. But I don't fault them for their fears, for it is my experience that in order to survive the great oceans, mariners must spread their five senses thinner than butter on a poor man's bread. This is especially true of whalers, as they are constantly on the lookout for spouters, so it is only natural for them to perceive signs of danger where others see none. The ocean is a strange place, and one we humans know too little of to claim to be masters of its secrets. Still, it was superstition that, in part, that lead to the *Absolom's* doom, and why I, alone, survived to tell this strange and fantastic tale. But I am getting ahead of myself.

How is it I have seawater in my veins, you ask? I came by it naturally enough, as my mother's eldest brother was once a whaler. As my Uncle Calvin was born early in my grandparent's marriage, and my mother late, there were as many years between brother and sister as are normally found between father and daughter. In any case, the difference in their ages did not weaken their familial bond, and when my uncle retired from the sea, he made his home with my mother and her family in Pennsylvania.

The decision to become landlocked was not of my Uncle Calvin's choosing, however, but one forced upon him. While returning from the Pacific whaling grounds, his ship was caught in a fierce storm that snapped the main mast like so much kindling. One of the spars collapsed across the deck, pinning my uncle underneath, costing him both legs below the knee. Luckily Uncle Calvin was the First Mate, and fortunate enough to ship with a captain who knew the whaling grounds like a bridegroom of fifty years knows his wife's backside, so he was able to retire with a goodly pension.

My memories of my uncle are fond ones. Every night he would sit by the fire and smoke his pipe, spinning yarns of his days on the open seas. He told stories of savage cannibals, wild dolphins sporting in the blue Pacific, and fighting typhoons in open water. While my brothers and sisters listened to these tales from a sense of duty, I was completely enthralled by his adventures. Uncle Calvin quickly saw in me a kindred spirit, and we became boon companions.

My family lived twenty-five miles outside the great city of Philadelphia. It was a pleasant enough place, I suppose, with its gently rolling hills and verdant pastures. It was bucolic and peaceful, the way all farming communities are, and completely lacking when it came to stimulating the imagination and passions of a young boy.

I know for a fact there was not single thing to be found in my hometown that could compare to the contents of my Uncle Calvin's sea chest. What wonders it held! Within its cedar-lined confines were such marvels as a shrunken human head and a dozen scrimshawed sperm whale teeth.

The most prized of my uncle's possessions, however, was not kept in his sea chest, but was worn about his neck. It was an amulet fashioned from a piece coral, carved in the shape of a dolphin. Its body was curved so that its nose touched the tip of its tail, and so perfect was the likeness, one could easily imagine it would swim away if placed in a pool of water. My Uncle claimed it was a good luck charm given to him by a native girl whose life he had once saved. The amulet was supposed to protect him from harm while at sea. Unfortunately, its powers had not extended to the air—or to ship's masts.

Despite my yearning to see the world, I would never have left home while my Uncle Calvin was still alive, for I had come to love him as my own grandfather, who died before I was born. But when his time came, my uncle left me three things: his sea chest, a letter of recommendation to a Captain Wendell Solomon, who he had known and called friend during his whaling days, and the dolphin amulet.

Suddenly, at the age of fifteen, I found myself free to answer the call that beckoned me since I was a small boy, seated by the family hearth, enthralled by tales of strange latitudes and stranger lands.

Chapter Two

My Arrival In Sag Harbor—The Blind Man Of Bay Street—The Whaler's Rest—I Am Re-Christened

Although many years have passed since the day I left home, and I have seen much in the way of the world, I shall never forget the day I first set foot in Sag Harbor.

Having grown up in a small village in Chester County, I was green as goose shit. But that didn't stop me from leaving home for one of the busiest seaports on the East Coast.

The first thing I saw as my coach drew within sight of Sag Harbor was a vast cluster of masts that towered above the rooftops like a mighty forest. As it was the first deep-water port on Long Island, over sixty whaling ships, not to mention countless other vessels, called it home. Because of this, the town's narrow streets teemed with people from places as far-flung as Fiji and the Ivory Coast.

There were more people walking up and down Division Street than in my entire hometown, and all of them were in a great hurry, as city people always seem to be. An African with skin black as pitch and raised tribal marking upon his face was haggling with an outfitter over the price of a kit, while next to him was a Sandwich Islander, his skin the color of buckwheat honey, with raven hair as sleek as the pelt of a seal, quietly studying a broadsheet posted on the wall of a nearby tavern. I approached an old man who was sharpening axes and harpoons from a makeshift tinker's stall built from canvas and wooden planking.

"Excuse me, sir..." I began.

The tinker looked up from his work and fixed me with an incurious stare, but did not halt his labors.

"I don't mean to take you from your work, my good sir, but could you tell me how to get to the harbor?"

The tinker gave a dry half-laugh and shook his head. "Don't you know nothing about this town, boy? All streets lead to the harbor! As long as you're headed north you'll eventually hit water."

I thanked the old man and followed the general flow of the foot traffic, which, as the tinker said, was northward bound. A hundred different languages could be heard with every step I took, and the closer I got to the water, the more alien and outlandish my surroundings became. At one point I saw an Algonquin Indian striding purposefully down the street, a steel-tipped harpoon clutched in his hand as if it was a walking stick, followed closely by a man with a piece of bone skewering his nose like the ring on a prize bull. After twenty minutes' walk, I finally reached the crowded warren of sail makers, grog shops, and brothels that comprised Bay Street.

The streets fronting the water were even more tightly packed than those I had walked earlier, and the air reeked of smoke from the nearby oil yards. For years I had yearned to see the exotic lands and people described so vividly to me by my beloved uncle, but I was still somewhat taken aback when faced with the reality of a whaling town. Being young and inexperienced, I was naturally hesitant to ask questions of any of these very strange strangers, so I set out to find someone who looked like they understood English and would not be tempted to eat me.

I spotted an elderly fellow dressed in the rough wool coat and watch cap of a mariner seated on a bench outside a tobacconist's. He was calmly smoking a pipe as the exotic denizens of Sag Harbor paraded past. He seemed old enough, and local enough, to possibly be able to answer my questions about the person I was looking for.

"Please pardon my intrusion, but could you possibly tell me where I might find a Captain Solomon?"

The old man tilted his head in my direction, so that I could see his face. With a start I realized his eyes were as blind as those of a baked fish. "Solly-man, is it?" The blind man drawled, taking the pipe from his mouth and giving it a hard rap against the edge of the bench. "He captains the *Absolom*, berthed on Long Wharf. Ye mean to go a'whalin', boy?"

"Yes, sir, I do."

"Are ye colored?" asked the blind man.

"No, sir."

"Then why sign on a whaler? It's hard, dirty, dangerous business. That's why most of the crews are darkies of some ilk or another. They'll work you like a slave, and by the time yer done ye'll owe more to the ship's store than ye can claim as a wage."

"You sound like you know something of it, my friend."

"I spent fifteen year in the foc'sle ," the blind man replied as his thumb and forefinger dipped into the tobacco pouch then quested about like sightless grubs until they found the warm heart of the bowl. "The bad air from the try-works affected the humors in me eyes. Struck me blind, it did."

"*Bilgewater!*" This was from a clerk dressed in a long white apron, a broom held in one hand, who stood in the doorway of the tobacco shop. "You went blind on account of gin, you old reprobate! And as for you, young man—if it's Wendell Solomon you're seekin', you stand as good a chance of findin' him in the Whaler's Rest than anywhere else in town." He pointed the broom handle at the tavern across the way, outside of which hung a sign made of crossed harpoons.

"How will I know him?"

"Oh, if he's in there, you'll find him soon enough!" The clerk replied with a laugh.

I thanked the shopkeeper and hurried across the street to the tavern. Up to that day, I had never once set foot in a place of drink, so you can imagine my surprise at what awaited me at the Whaler's Rest.

The interior was crammed to the rafters with a wild mélange of humanity, most of whom seemed to either be from some far-off country or missing some part of their anatomy, if not both, and all of whom were talking at the top of their lungs. The pipe smoke was so thick I could have cut it with a knife and used it for chaw. The sawdust that covered the rough plank floor was composed of equal parts vomit and urine, mainly because those patrons not drinking, talking or smoking were slumped across tables or stretched out in pools of their own waste.

As I looked about the crowd of unfamiliar faces scattered about the tavern's central room, I despaired of ever being able to locate Captain Solomon. Then I heard a laugh so strong and powerful it cut through the surrounding din like Moses parting the Red Sea. Upon hearing that laugh I realized I had found my man.

Although I have met many a mariner since that day, Wendell Solomon remains, to my mind, the perfect specimen of a sea captain. Even in a bar filled with Red Indians and cannibal Maori, this native Long Islander cut quite the figure. He was six-foot-four, if he stood an inch, with shoulders as wide as an oar. His face was as weathered as a light-housekeeper's watch-shack, framed by a great mass of black hair streaked white at the temples, with matching marks in his beard. His right eye was as blue as a robin's egg and as clear as the sky over Eden, while the left was covered with a patch of plain black cloth. He stood with his back to the bar, facing the door, and was dressed in a pair of black wool pants and a gray cable sweater, his cap pulled low on his brow as he drank from a pewter tankard.

I stepped forward and coughed into my fist, doing my best to control the anxiety in my voice. "Beg pardon, sir—but might you be Captain Solomon?"

"That depends on who's doin' the askin'," the sea captain replied, fixing me with his one good eye. "Do I know ye, boy?"

"No, sir. But I believe you knew my late uncle, Calvin Jenkins. He gave me this letter of recommendation and said I should present it to you, or to any captain I might meet, should you happen to be dead."

The distrust in Solomon's eye dimmed, to be replaced with a warmer humor as he took the letter from me. He opened it, glanced at the handwriting, and then returned his solitary stare to my face. "So, you're Cal's nephew, eh? I remember him sayin' he had family Philadelphia way. And you have a bit of his look about you. Well, son, truth to tell—your uncle was one of the bravest men I ever set sail with, and that's sayin' some. Back when we was on the old *Mount Vernon*, I once seen him rescue a native girl from a shark—leapt right off the deck, he did, and landed on the monster's back! It was a big, mean bastard, but damned if he didn't stab it to death as easy as you please! So, boy, even if you're but a hair on your uncle's ass, you'll still make a worthy addition to my crew."

"So you'll take me?"

"Did I not just say as much? My ship is the *Absolom*. She's anchored on the Long Wharf—you'll know her by her figurehead: a gilded eagle. My second, Mr. Shreve, is handling the signing-on." He fished a pencil stub from the pocket of his coat and took the envelope containing my uncle's letter and made a mark upon it, then handed it back. "Show this to him— he'll know what to do."

"Thank you, Captain Solomon!" I beamed. "You won't regret it!"

"Aye," he said with a nod and wry half-smile. "We'll see if you're still thankin' me a year in from today, eh?"

Strolling down the aptly-named Long Wharf was like walking down a city street where all the houses just happened to have masts and anchor chains. Where the streets of Sag Harbor were a mass of swirling chaos to my young eyes, the Long Wharf had a definite sense of order and purpose to its madness.

Teamsters drove up and down the length of the wharf, making deliveries of everything from sailcloth to crates of live chickens. Scores of coopers, caulkers, and carpenters set up shop alongside their respective ships as they worked, while longshoremen hurried up and down the gangplanks, loading or unloading the holds as necessary.

It did not take me long to find the *Absolom*. The sun reflected off the gilded eagle fixed to her prow, causing it to flash as brightly as an ancient warrior's shield. As I drew closer, I spied a man standing near the gangplank, studying a ledger propped open on a wooden cask. He was short and stout, like the stump of a mighty oak, with a neck as thick as a bull's and hair the color of a ginger cat. His complexion was the permanent sunburn you find on fair-skinned folk who work in the open elements.

"Are you Mr. Shreve?"

The stump-like man raised pale green eyes from the ledger and nodded. When he spoke, his voice was surprisingly light and musical. "That I am."

"Captain Solomon said I should show this to you," I said, handing him the marked envelope.

Shreve frowned at the captain's scribble for a long moment, raised a single eyebrow, and removed the letter, being careful not to tear the paper as he unfolded it. I was impressed by the delicacy of movement and voice in a man who seemed so outwardly blunt.

"Cal Jenkins! That's a name I haven't heard in a month of Sundays! I knew your uncle, I did. Not as well as the Cap'n. Him and Cal went back a-ways, to hear the tale. But I shipped with him. It was my first voyage and his last. What? Twelve years ago? I couldn't have been much older than you are now. I was one of the men who helped hold him down when the ship's carpenter took his legs off—or, at least what was left of them. So, boy—what is your name?"

"Padgett. Jonah Padgett."

Shreve's joviality disappeared as quickly as chalk wiped from a slate. "Is it, now?"

"Is there a problem, Mr. Shreve?"

"Sailors are a superstitious lot, lad, what with most of them being heathens of some sort. Jonah is a bad name for a sailor to have; especially a whaler. From here on in, boy, if you want to bunk on the *Absolom*, or any ship for that matter, your name is *Jonas*, is that clear?"

"Aye, sir. That it is."

"Good lad!" Shreve said, his previous good humor returning as quickly as it had disappeared. "Now, do you claim any skill beyond that of a strong back?"

"My father runs a mill," I replied. "I helped him make the casks and barrels that held the flour."

"Excellent! Our tight cooper is in sore need of an apprentice, as he lost the last one to snail fever. Come make your mark in the books, and I'll put you down for your share."

I did as I was bid, being careful to spell my new name correctly in the ship's ledger. Mr. Shreve smiled broadly and gave me a clap on the back that would make a mule stagger.

"Welcome aboard the *Absolom*, boyo! You're lucky you caught us, when you did. This is our last day at dock. We set sail for the Pacific hunting grounds in the morning!"

Chapter Three

A Final Farewell—The Crew Of The *Absolom*—The Forecastle—Captain Solomon At The Rail

As the first rays of the rising sun touched its rigging, the *Absolom* pulled up anchor and slipped into the falling tide that flowed into Gardiner's Bay. As we passed Montauk's rounded bluff, several of the crew, including Captain Solomon and his mates, gathered along the rail. The swearing, laughing and spitting that had seemed so much a part of their collective nature as breathing was replaced by a deep and sudden silence. Curious, I joined their number.

"What are we looking at?" This I asked of Mr. Shreve, who, at this point, had proven himself the most accessible of the mates.

"See that, boyo?" he said in a hushed voice, pointing to the lighthouse situated high atop the bluff. "It's the last any of us will see of Long Island for the next year or three—and, in all probability, there's one or two of us who will ne'er see it again."

I thought about what he had said for a moment, and then gave a sidelong glance to the faces ranged along the rail. Although each man's eye was riveted on the distant lighthouse, I could tell each was seeing something different, be it the face of a sweetheart, child, or beloved mother. No wonder those gathered at the rail were as quiet as churchmen.

Perhaps now is as good a time as any to describe to you the crew whose lives and space I shared aboard the *Absolom*. On a whaler, all the men must rely on one another and work as a team. Yet there remains a very strict social order at work, as rigid as that of the Hindoos.

The highest position held on board was, of course, that of the captain. Below him were his four mates, then the four master harpooners. These nine men slept in special quarters, each set aside for their own station, in the ship's stern, and fed at the captain's table. Next came the craftsmen, those whose jobs were to keep the day-to-day of the ship on an even keel: the cooper, the blacksmith, the cook, and the steward, who slept amidships and dined on fare less than that of the captain's table, but far better than what was served to the deckhands, who shared the cramped and foul confines of the bow. Despite our keeping such close quarters, or perhaps because of it, there was even a hierarchy to be found amongst the deckhands, with the old salts having an advantage over the green hands, regardless of the color of their skin.

The Captain and Second Mate of the *Absolom* I have already described. I shall attempt to do justice to the others, in descending order of rank.

The First Mate, Mr. Godward, was a long, tall drink of water that walked with his shoulders drawn up and his hands clasped behind his back. He reminded me of a stork, wading its way through the shallows. When he was not standing watch, he served as the ship's pilot. Although he was lean in build, his hands were strong enough to snap a harpoon lance in two. A New Bedfordman, he kept his own council and watched the carryings on of the crew with a flinty eye. Where, in my mind, Captain Solomon embodied the very sea itself, Mr. Godward personified the craggy shore the surf crashed against.

The Third Mate, Mr. Levant, was an outwardly unremarkable sort, save for two attributes. The first was a pair of bushy eyebrows that swept outward, like the wings of a bat, shielding the sharpest eyes ever set into a human skull. In the harshest glare from the westering sun, he could spot the flash of a fluke from a league away, aided, in no small part, by the shade thrown by those magnificent brows. The second attribute were the two missing fingers of his left hand, the digits in question having been severed in an accident with a whale-line.

The ship's Bos'un was Mr. Gusset, whose charge it was to oversee the cleaning and maintenance of the *Absolom* while at sea and at dock. He was a broad-shouldered fellow with tattoos of crossed anchors on each forearm. His huge hands belied a surprising delicacy with needle and thread, which he used to mend the sails and sew-up the occasional crewman.

As for the harpooners, they were a motley lot, their single unifying feature being their prodigious size and skill with the long iron. One man was assigned to each of the four boats under the command of the ship's officers. The first harpooner, the one who hurled his iron from the captain's boat, was a strapping Swede named Haraldson, whose blonde brows were so sun-bleached they were all but invisible to the naked eye.

The second harpooner, who manned the First Mate's boat, was the African, Mulogo. Mulogo was without a doubt the tallest man I have ever clapped eyes on; and to my dying day I will carry the image of him standing in the gunwale of his longboat, framed against the blue sky of the Pacific like an ebony watchtower poised on a lonesome cliff.

The third and fourth harpooners were a pair of runaway slaves named Virgil and Homer, who were jokingly referred to as "The Classics" by the rest of the crew. At first it was difficult for me to tell the one from the other, until I noticed that Virgil bore deep scarring across his right shoulder, and that Homer still wore the remnant of a manacle as a grim keepsake on his left ankle.

As for the craftsmen, the ship's cooper was a Portugee by the name of Santo. The blacksmith, who was also in charge of the ship's try-works, went by the name of Cuppy. He was easily the oldest man on board the *Absolom*, with snowy white hair and beard, and a small and wiry build, save for his massive arms, which were as big around at the bicep as a young girl's thigh. He reminded me of the god Vulcan, whose crippled frame hid prodigious strength and stamina.

The cook, if he could be so called, was a fellow named Pedro, who claimed to be from Peru. For all I know he was a wizard in the galley, but you not could prove it by what he served me. While the captain, mates, harpooners, and the ship's craftsmen were fed on beef, fowl, and the like, the rest of us had to make do with jerked beef, cold coffee, watery stew and sea biscuits hard enough to drive a nail through an oaken plank.

This now brings me to my fellow crewmen—and a strange and unlikely lot they were, too. At least half were Negroes and Red Indians of various hues, the rest an odd mixture of Yankees, South-Sea Islanders, and Europeans. Of the white men, no matter what their nationality, they could easily be divided into three categories: those who were born to sea-faring families; romantics seeking adventure; and escaped convicts. Of the three, I fell into the middle category, much to the amusement of the former and the disgust of the latter.

My uncle had told me stories of just how hard the life of a whaling man could be, but in my childish fascination I had chosen to ignore them in favor of the tales of cannibal attacks and native princesses. Imagine my dismay when I was shown what would be my home for the next year or more—a narrow, triangle-shaped room located under the deck in the bow of the ship, known as the forecastle or foc'sle.

It was only accessible by a single hatch on the top deck, and was otherwise without windows or doors. It was dark and the walls were literally black with slime and filth. Even in the milder climates the foc'sle could be uncomfortably hot, but in the heat of the Pacific it became a virtual oven reeking of seawater, sweat, smoke, vomit, farts, piss and sperm—in short, it smelled of men in too-close quarters under horrid conditions. The crew slept in narrow wooden bunks that lined the walls, and the only place a deckhand had to sit was on his own sea chest.

Since the foc'sle was at the front of the ship, it took the brunt of the waves, much to the discomfort of the green hands—myself included—who spent the first few days of the outward journey attempting to get their sea-legs.

As we lay in our hard bunks, spewing vomit with every pitch and roll of the storm-tossed ship, the more seasoned salts smoked, laughed, and chatted amongst themselves. The only time they would acknowledge our existence was by cursing us whenever they slipped in a puddle of sick. Although, at the time, I could not find the humor in my situation, I have since come to see myself through the eyes of the old salts whose berth I shared, and I must admit that I was, indeed, a fool.

Still, as horrid as conditions in the foc'sle were, they were counterbalanced by the beauty and majesty of the sea herself. Each morning, as I clambered out of the stinking darkness, the merest sliver of blue was all it took to raise my spirits and spur me onto the deck to greet the day.

The first few weeks out of Long Island en route to the whaling grounds of the Pacific were uneventful, in the sense that we were not expected to hunt whales. Instead, the time was spent shaking down the crew, training the green hands in what was expected of them, and doing last-minute repairs and preparations to the ship before the hunt began in earnest. At the time I thought I was worked far harder than any white man could stand, but would soon discover that what I fancied was a bed of hot coals was really a feather mattress.

One evening, as I was keeping watch from the deck, I caught wind of the smell of burning tobacco coming from behind me. I turned to find Captain Solomon standing at the rail. Save for the occasional glimpse of him as he went in and out of his cabin, this was the first time I had been within striking distance of the man since out initial meeting at the Whaler's Rest.

"So, young Padgett," he said, the words coming out accompanied by puffs of fragrant smoke. "How do you find the life of a sailor?"

"I-I find it good, sir," I managed to stammer out.

Solomon looked at me, so I could see that he knew he had caught me in a falsehood, and smiled with the half of his mouth not busy with his clay pipe. "Is that the truth?"

"It isn't exactly a lie, sir," I replied. "The food is awful, the work is hard, my bed reeks of sick, and I fear half of the men I share my berth are as likely to kill me in my sleep as look at me. But this…" I pointed to the open water and sky laid out before me like a splendid mirror. "This is as good as the Lord makes it."

"By damn, you *do* have Cal's blood in you!" Solomon said with a chuckle. "He was one for speakin' his heart, no matter who was listenin'. You do realize, don't you, son, that most of what you just said could get your back painted with stripes?

Still, I can respect a man who says his mind. And your mind, it seems, ain't so far from my own.

"I've witnessed all manner of things in my day, lad: I seen crocodiles and sharks fight to the death in the mouth of the Nile, and tigers swimmin' in the moonlight in the Bay of Bengal. I seen a squid the size of a frigate clamped in the jaws of a sperm, and a Great White swaller a man in one gulp, like he was an oyster on the half-shell. Strange and terrible things they were, indeed. And I reckon there's as much death and suffering on the land as there is on the water. But I never did see anything on dry land that compares to the sun setting in the Pacific.

"I'm not a poet, boy. And God knows I'm no philosopher. But I reckon, if he's lucky, at some point in his life a man knows where he's supposed to be. And I'm supposed to be out here—and perhaps you are, too."

With that, Captain Solomon removed the pipe from his mouth, gave it a light rap against the railing, so that the bowl's contents emptied into the water below, and strolled back to his cabin.

Chapter Four

The Hunt Off Valparaiso—Man Overboard—Bloody Work— King Jim—What Stood Upon The Whale

I engaged in my first whale hunt just off the coast of Uruguay, but I will not bore you with the re-telling of every time I set chase after the great sea beasts, for, in fact, every pursuit is near identical to the one before and the one after it. And all hunts end in either one of two ways: either a whale is caught, or it is not. However, I will describe to you the hunt that cost us the first harpooner, for it leads, in part, to the final fate of the *Absolom*. We were four months out of Sag Harbor, cruising the waters off Valparaiso before making the long trek to the Marquesas Islands, when it happened. By that point I had three chases and two kills under my belt, and had already developed a taste for the thrill of the hunt. The killing and rendering of whales, especially the toothed variety, is very hard and dangerous work, but preferable to the drudgery of life onboard a whaler when there are no spouters to be seen.

I was scrubbing down the deck when I heard Mr. Levant, he of the prodigious eyebrows, sing out: *"Thar she blows!"*

Mr. Godward, whose watch it was, came forward. *"Where away?"* he called in response.

"Off the port bow!"

As a man, the crew dropped whatever they were doing and raced to the left hand rails, eagerly scanning the horizon for the tell-tale plume of spray that marked the passing of their prey.

Captain Solomon emerged from his cabin at the ship's

stern, spyglass in hand. He raised it to his good eye, and after a second's study a wide grin wreathed his mouth. "It's a pod, by damn! There's six, perhaps more, of the beasties!" With a whoop, he turned and grabbed the clapper of the watch bell mounted outside his door and began ringing it like preacher calling his congregation to prayer. *"To your boats, men! To your boats!"*

With that all hell broke loose, as every man on deck, and those below, scrambled to take his place at the long boats, which hung in eternal readiness from davits alongside the ship. Each boat was sleek, double-ended, and thirty-feet long, outfitted with harpoons, lances, knives, and axes, as well as bailing buckets, emergency rations, a knock-down sail, and provisions.

Each boat housed six men: the header, the harpooner, and four oarsmen. Early during our voyage out, the captain and his mates had put the green hands through their paces, divvying us up amongst them as they saw fit. Thanks to my uncle's tutelage in the manufacture of knots, I found myself assigned to Captain Solomon's boat. My fellow oarsmen consisted of an Orkneyman named Jones, a mulatto called Nicodemus, and a West Indian who went by Marcus. Our harpooner was the Swede, Haraldson.

While there was much about the *Absolom* that did not live up to my romantic notions of the whaling life, the harpooners were one of the few that did not disappoint. I was particularly impressed by Haraldson. AAlthough he did not speak to me, I knew he wanted to show me something and I leapt from the boat without a moment's hesitation.

He was jovial in nature and fond of dancing the hornpipe while playing the ocarina, when he was not sharpening his harpoon with a whetstone, and his booming laugh was as loud and as vital as that of the captain. As the Swede was naturally fair, years of exposure to the sun had bleached his hair whiter than cotton, while imparting a tan so deep his skin looked like seasoned leather. With his face framed by two thick braids and decorated by a flowing mustache, he looked every inch the Viking lords from whom he claimed descent.

One by one the long boats were dropped into the water,

each laden with men and equipment. I took my place at the oars, while Captain Solomon seated himself at the tiller and Haraldson took the short seat behind the bow. All I could see of the hunt was the backs of the men seated in front of me and the face of Captain Solomon. As the boat header, it was his job to keep our prey in sight and steer the long boat in its direction. As our backs were to the whale, none of us would know if we were within striking distance of our prey until the captain sang out for the harpooner to stand or, if we were unlucky, the great beast smashed our boat with one of its flukes.

"Faster, men!" Captain Solomon shouted, over the constant hiss and slap of the waves. "She sounded half an hour ago! She'll be coming up for breath sooner than not!"

I put all thoughts of pain and weariness out of my mind and focused instead on the task at hand. Once you are out in the boats on the open ocean, allowing your concentration to wander for even the briefest moment is an invitation to death and disaster.

Foremost in my mind was the desire to stay clear of the whale line, which lay coiled in a tub near the rear of the boat. The far end of the rope was attached to the harpoon stowed in the bow of the boat, then looped around the wooden loggerhead beside the tiller, to provide enough tension to tire the whale. Once the harpoon was fixed in its target, the rope stretched itself tight along the line of the keel, between the oarsmen, and over the bow into the water. It was the Bos'n's business to see that the whale rope was perfectly coiled within its tub, for fear of the slightest kink in the rope catching on the boat and dragging us under. If that was not reason enough to stay clear of the damned thing, if a crewman was careless and got in the way of the unwinding rope, he would find himself instantly entangled and yanked overboard. Or, since the rope moved so quickly and without slack, he would easily lose a finger or thumb, as the line sliced through flesh and bone as easily as a knife.

So there we were, out on the open ocean, under a merciless Chilean sun, rowing until our backs cracked, with the *Absolom* trailing after us like a curious onlooker, until we reached the spot where Captain Solomon predicted our prey would surface.

We sat there, wordlessly, hunched over our oars, as our boat bobbed atop the water, while our leader scanned the surface for sign of rising whale. A mile to either side of us the boats piloted by Mr. Godward and Mr. Levant kept their own watch, while Mr. Shreve's boat stayed behind an equal distance. After what seemed to be half an eternity, I saw the smile of a hunter whose patience has been rewarded break across the captain's face.

"Row! Row, you bastards! She's coming up starboard!"

There was a deep rumble, from both beneath and above the waves, as hundreds of tons of water were rapidly displaced, and suddenly the sperm whales were amongst us. One of the great beasts broke the surface of the water not a hundred yards from us, rising like a new-born island from the ocean floor. A geyser shot upwards, showering us with thick droplets of hot vapor, as if Neptune himself had let out a mighty gasp.

"Stand!" Captain Solomon shouted over the clamor of the whale.

Although I could not see him, I heard Haraldson put aside his oars and stand to brace himself in the bow. I glanced over at the nearest boat, which was closing in as fast as it could on its own whale, and saw in the figure of Mulogo a mirror of the Swede's actions as he lifted the harpoon from its resting place. Each harpooner had to stand in the front of the heaving boat and propel the heavy, single-flue iron spear with enough force to plant it deep in the whale's back. Should the harpooner miss on his first strike, he then had to reel the weapon, hand-over-hand, back into the boat, and try again before the beast sounded once again.

"Stern all!" Captain Solomon bellowed as Haraldson's iron bit deep into its target.

As my fellow oarsmen changed positions in order to back the boat away from the whale's flukes, the boat struck something unseen beneath the waves—exactly what will never be known—causing the Swede to lose his balance and stumble into the whale line. One moment he was there, the next he was jerked from the bow like a marionette from a puppet stage.

There was no time for mourning the harpooner, though, as the great sea beast, enraged by pain and fear, began to run, dragging line, boat and crew behind it like a child trailing a kite. When it found it could not escape by fleeing, it sounded, diving deep into the deepest reaches of the sea.

We fought against the wounded creature, hauling on the line until our muscles screamed and our nerves caught fire. Our prey struggled mightily, but, in the end, it could not stay down. Although shaped like a fish, the whale, just like man, must breathe air to survive.

"Ahoy, laddies!" the captain shouted, as the whale rope began to slacken. "She's comin' up to see us!"

My fellow oarsmen and I began frantically hauling the whale line in hand-over-hand, trying to shorten the distance between us and our prey once it surfaced. Just then the whale arose before us, causing the boat to sharply rise then slap back down, nearly sending me tumbling into the churning water.

"Yo, Padgett!" Captain Solomon shouted, slapping my sunburned shoulder as he moved from the back of the boat to take Haraldson's place in the bow. "Keep us steady!"

I clambered to the rear of the boat and grabbed the tiller, which struggled in my grip like a living thing. From my new vantage point, I could see the toothed whale not fifty feet from where I sat, the Swede's harpoon jutting from its gleaming hide like a needle stuck in a pincushion.

Captain Solomon took up Haraldson's second iron and with a mighty bellow let it fly. The harpoon struck the whale and held fast. With a flash of its flukes, the sperm swam away and we were once more dragged along on a wild sleigh-ride, leaving our fellows—and the *Absolom*—far behind before it once more sounded beneath the waves.

During the hour we waited for the whale to rise, Mr. Levant's boat finally rejoined us, although Mr. Shreve and Mr. Godward were nowhere to be seen. By the time our prey resurfaced, it was evident the beast was considerably weakened. Captain Solomon ordered us to close in on the animal and took up a long, spear-like lance, which he plunged, again and again, into the exhausted animal's vitals.

The whale gave voice to a sound few human ears have known, but once heard can never be forgotten, followed by a burst of blood from it spout, which coated everyone in the boat in fresh gore.

"Hurrah, Cap'n!" Mr. Levant shouted from his boat. "You've tapped the claret!"

"That I have!" Solomon agreed as he resumed his place as header. "Now lets put some distance between us, lads! We haven't chased this black devil this long and hard just to get smashed to kindling in its death flurry!"

I returned to my seat and began rowing for my life, the dolphin amulet thumping against my breastbone like a doorknocker with every stroke. The last few minutes of a doomed whale's life are the most dangerous to those who hunt them. Many a sailor has met his end from the wildly flailing fluke at the end of a hunt.

Once we were safely away, we rested on our oars and watched as the sperm whale swam violently about in ever decreasing circles, until it had churned the sea into a foamy, bloody chaos. After a half hour of this, the stricken beast abruptly began to beat the water with its tail and then gave a huge shudder. A ragged cheer rang out from our boat and Mr. Levant's as the creature turned fin-out, rolling over on its side. However, our rejoicing proved short-lived, as we were now faced with the daunting task of towing the massive carcass back to the ship.

Jones the Orkneyman stood up and fished the whale lines out of the water with a boat hook, one of which was secured to our boat, the other to Mr. Levant's. Then, after a brief break for fresh water and a meal of hardtack, we began the long, arduous task of rowing back to the *Absolom*, dragging our kill behind us like a hound bringing home a dead rabbit for its master. The ship, which had been following us from a distance, now sat waiting on the horizon, left motionless by a change in the winds

It was during the return journey, towing forty tons of deadweight, that the sharks showed up. They arose from the depths like shadows, summoned by the blood of the slain behemoth, their dorsal fins breaking the surface like a knife slitting a throat.

While it was not uncommon for these vultures of the sea to serve as grim escort to a butchered whale, I was surprised to see so many appear at once, for sharks are not social animals, like dolphins or whales. There were easily twenty or more of the dreadful beasts darting through the water, snatching mouthfuls of flesh from the carcass like greedy children trying to steal pies cooling on a window sill.

To my horror, one of the damned things swam up to the whale boat and clamped its fearsome jaws about the flat of my oar, as if trying to yank it from my grip. From what I could see of it, it was what the Maori call a mako, with a pointy snout and relatively short dorsal fin and overlarge, circular eyes as black and flat as shoebuttons.

Suddenly a lance-like spear stabbed down over my shoulder and into shark's face, striking it in the eye. The mako surrendered its hold on the oar and dove back below the surface, leaving a trail of blood to mark its passing.

"Accursed things!" Captain Solomon spat as he resumed his place at the tiller and tucked the lance—the same one he had used to kill the whale—back into its storage space. "We'll be lucky they don't take a third of the carcass before we finish the cutting-in."

After three hours of hard rowing, we finally made it back to the *Absolom*. We brought our catch to the starboard side, and the whale line affixed to each boat was untied and attached to a pulley lowered from above. The carcass was then winched into place by its tail and secured to the side of the boat.

Mr. Levant's harpooner, Homer, leapt out of his boat, his manacle rattling as he clambered across the slippery back of the dead whale, heedless of the sharks that swarmed the water below, while a cutting stage fashioned from three heavy planks was lowered over the carcass. The former slave cut a hole in the skin and blubber near the whale's eye and inserted a hook connected though a series of ropes and pulleys to the ship's windlass, so that the body was fastened, head and tail, to the *Absolom*.

Then, and only then, was a rope ladder tossed over the railing, allowing the crews of the whaleboats back on aboard.

"Where be Godward and Shreve?" Captain Solomon called out to Gusset as he cleared the rail.

"They was headed west after a spouter before the wind quit us, sir," the bo'sun reported.

"Even if our sails were full, we can't go looking for them until we've finished the cutting-in," Solomon grunted, staring in the direction of the lowering sun.

While the captain and the bo'sun discussed the whereabouts of the other whaleboats, I and the others made a bee-line to the water casks to quench our thirst. After six hours on the open sea, I was burned red as a lobster in the pot, and my skin was peeling away from my shoulders and arms like that of an onion. Still, despite a full day spent behind the oars, we were allowed only the briefest of rests in the shade of the mast, where we were served a meal of salted beef and cold coffee, before being ordered to begin the bloody work of rendering the whale.

Nicodemus and Marcus took up a pair of long-handled cutting spades and shimmied down the ropes to the cutting stage atop the carcass. There they cut in to the blubber, slicing blanket pieces five feet wide and fifteen feet long, ten inches thick. Then Marcus boarded the body and fixed a huge hook into the swath they had just cut, which was then peeled off the carcass using the windlass and hoisted aboard, dripping oil and blood down upon the deck and deckhands alike.

As I watched in disgust and amazement, Marcus then turned and let fly with a stream of piss on the multitude of sharks not ten feet from where he stood atop the whale, laughing in contempt at the fearsome scavengers as they swarmed the carcass like farrow nursing off the teats of a sow.

When the two blocks of the tackle finally came together and no rope remained to lift it higher, the blanket-piece was sliced away and lowered into the blubber room in the upper hold near the main hatch. There it was cut into smaller horse-pieces of four feet by six inches, and then reduced further still into 'bible leaves', which were taken back on deck and fed into the copper try-pots set atop the furnaces affixed between the foremast and the mainmast, in order to be boiled into oil.

My job was to assist Santo, the ship's cooper, in making the barrels used to store the precious cargo, and insure they were securely sealed before being stowed in the hold. Santo was a rotund fellow, not unlike the barrels he built, with a silver ring in one ear. He was what they called a tight cooper, who made casks for long-term storage and transportation of liquids.

Although Santo did not speak much English—and I spoke no Portuguese at all—I found his company agreeable, and the same seemed to hold true for him. To tell the truth, even if the man had been the devil himself, I would have still counted myself lucky to work by his side, as the ship's cooperage was far preferable to toiling in the dark, reeking confines of the blubber room or skimming the skin and tissue from the hissing, spitting try-pots.

We labored hard for the rest of the day as the blazing sun gradually sank into the horizon, like a fresh-forged sword being quenched in a blacksmith's bath. It was then one of the crewmen sang out from the crow's nest.

"Long boat off the port bow!"

The crew on deck stopped what they were doing to hurry to the rail, to see what looked to be Mr. Shreve's boat making its way back to the *Absolom* like a chick headed for the protection of the mother hen.

"Where's Mr. Godward and his men?" I asked.

Mr. Gusset took out a spyglass and squinted at the approaching boat. "The First Mate's in the whale boat with Shreve, along with Mulogo," he replied solemnly. "I don't see any of the others from his boat."

As Mr. Shreve put alongside the *Absolom*, and its crew was taken up out of the sea, Captain Solomon pushed his way through the men gathered on the deck, cursing and kicking those who did not get out of his way fast enough. "Get back to your stations!" he barked. "Have you dogs never seen a whale boat come back empty-handed from a hunt before?" He then turned to face his First Mate, who stood before him, shivering as if the grip of fever."What happened, Mr. Godward?"

"Mulongo sank his harpoon into this nice fat cow on his first throw," the Mate replied. "She started to run—but wheeled about when her calf couldn't keep up. That's when Mulongo got the second iron in her. Then, suddenly, this bull sperm whale—the largest I've ever seen, with skin black as the devil's eyes—breached beside us and stove in the boat with a flick of his tail. The next thing I know, Mulongo has his arm about me and is swimming as fast as he can for Shreve's whale boat. As for the others…none of them came back up." A look of horror crossed Godward's face, as if part of him was still back in the water. "I've never seen a monster like it before. It had to be him, Cap'n—it was King Jim."

A muttering arose from the assembled crew, spurring Captain Solomon to snatch the cat from his belt and angrily strike at those sailors unlucky enough to be closest at hand. "What are you, whalers or old women?" he thundered. "I said get back to work!"

Mr. Levant and Mr. Gusset took up the captain's line, cursing and shouting at the crew to get back to their stations, or run the risk of a flogging. The sailors grumbled but returned to work as the Captain hurried Godward and Mulogo into his cabin for what I can only assume to be further inquisition.

As Santo and I returned to his cooperage, I ventured a question as to this 'King Jim' that seemed to worry the crew so much.

"King Jim is big fish," the Portugee replied. "Very big, very *angry* fish."

"You mean a whale?"

"*Sim, a maior das baleia,*" he said solemnly. "Some say King Jim devil. Some say god. I think both."

"That's blasphemy," I pointed out as judiciously as I could.

"*Sim,*" the cooper conceded. "The earth and the sky, that belongs to God. But the ocean? The ocean belongs to King Jim."

There is nothing filthier than the trying out of a whale. It is ceaseless, backbreaking work that goes on day and night until the last of the blubber is melted down in the copper cauldrons of the try-works. During this time the crew ends up working like horses, their days spent in grueling six-hour shifts, and living like pigs, as there is no point in cleaning oneself until the last drop of oil is poured into the final barrel, and the try-pots thoroughly scoured.

Everything, and I mean *everything*, is coated in oil during the trying-out process. It rises in thick, reeking plumes from the boiling pots, covering everything from the decks to the sails to the sailors themselves in a foul, greasy sheen. It even permeates the foodstuffs and the eating utensils, so that everything smells and tastes of blubber. It is made even worse by the fact that the fires beneath the try-works are fed not with wood, but with those pieces of whale deemed unsuitable for the boiling pots. As a result, there is literally nowhere onboard where one can escape the fetid odor of burning, boiling or raw, rotting whale.

It was around midnight when Mr. Gusset told Santo and me to close up shop and get some sleep. We had made over twenty barrels that day and, after a few hours rest, would make twenty more.

As weary as I was, the idea of heading down to the stinking, dank fo'csle was enough to make my stomach cinch itself into a sheepshank. I decided to take a walk around the top deck, in vain hope of catching a breath of fresh air, but instead found myself staring down over the starboard railing at what was left of the behemoth I had helped kill.

In the flickering, orangish light cast by the try-works, I could see that all the blubber had been stripped from the carcass, and all that remained was for the whale to be decapitated in order to harvest the precious, high-grade spermaceti it carried about in its skull case. I looked around, but the flensers were nowhere to be seen—no doubt they had gone to exchange their cutting spades for the longer, heavier head spades used to chop through the vertebrae in the whale's neck.

From where I stood, I could hear the threshing of the sharks in the water below as they fought amongst themselves for the choicest morsels of flesh. Their ceaseless feeding reminded of me of maggots working to reduce a corpse.

Just then I saw the figure of a naked man emerge from the shark-infested water and clamber up onto the back of the skint whale. At first my exhausted mind thought Haraldson, the lost harpooner, had somehow miraculously escaped drowning, man-eating sharks and the open sea and found his way back to the *Absolom*. But then I realized that the figure was utterly devoid of hair and had a noticeably hunched back. Whoever—or whatever—it was walking across the dead whale it most certainly was not the Swede.

As I watched in stunned silence, the hunched figure—still dripping from the ocean—fell to his knees and began tearing at the exposed, rotting meat with his bare hands, stuffing the gobbets of flesh into his mouth. I cried out in horror and disgust, instinctively clutching the amulet about my neck for protection.

The figure crouched atop the whale's carcass suddenly jerked his head in my direction, revealing a gaping maw full of jagged teeth and what were clearly gill slits along the sides of his neck. The glow of the try-works cast a flickering light on its left eye—which was as round and black as a shoe-button—while revealing the right to be a gouged, red ruin.

Part Two

Blood on the Beach

Chapter Five

My Eyes Deceived—Sea Changes Amongst The Crew—Nuka Hiva—A Shadow In The Surf—My Uncle's Secret

Upon seeing the face of the horror that knelt atop the whale, I cried out in alarm and fled the rail. Without thinking, I ran to awaken Santo, who slept in a hammock strung up in the ship's cooperage, and informed him of what I had seen crawl out of the shark-infested sea.

"You are *louco* for no sleep," he snarled, unappreciative of having been shaken from his well-earned slumber. "That why you see *sereia*."

"But it's not a mermaid!" I protested. "It's something else—something like a shark, but it walks like a man! And it's real, I tell you!"

"Go sleep, Jonas, before I hit you," Santo grumbled, turning his back to me.

I did not dare try to rouse my friend a second time, for fear he would make good on his threat. So I returned starboard and cautiously peered over the rail at the whale carcass tethered to the *Absolom's* side. Although the water was still full of hungry sharks, the grotesque, one-eyed creature was nowhere to be seen. In its place were a pair of deckhands working diligently from their perches on the cutting platform to separate the deceased sperm's lower jaw and head from the rest of the body. Judging by their blasé manner as they sawed away at the leviathan's neck, neither recently seen anything as untoward as a human shark.

I rubbed my weary eyes and shook my head in reproof. Santo was right: I was so tired I was hallucinating. If I didn't get some rest, I would soon be seeing angels nesting in the riggings and sea serpents frolicking off the port bow.

Both relieved and embarrassed by this revelation, I returned to my lowly, stinking bunk in the foc'sle. Despite the sound of the sharks thumping against the hull of the ship as they continued their ceaseless feeding, I quickly fell into a deep and, mercifully, dreamless slumber.

The weeks following the untimely death of Haraldson proved sad ones for all who shipped the *Absolom*. But his absence was felt most keenly by those of us in the Captain's boat. Although Jones the Orkneyman and Marcus took turns in the bow, neither proved to have the Swede's keen eye and sure hand when it came to the tossing of harpoons.

One would not think it difficult to land a strike against the broadside of something the size of a whale, but more times than not their throws ended up in the drink and had to be reeled back into the boat as fast as possible, before our prey returned to the safety of the depths.

Where once we had hunted down our share of whale, now we found ourselves, more often than not, assisting the other boats in their kills, instead of making our own. Although the pay of a whaling man is decided by the sum of the ship's cargo, there is a tally kept of which officer's boat was responsible for what kills, and bonuses applied to the most productive teams, going from greater to lesser, and where once the Captain's boat was at the top of the list, now it was squarely on the bottom.

But as disconcerting as Haraldson's death may have been for the crew of the *Absolom*, it was nothing compared to the sea-change Mr. Godward underwent following his tragic encounter with the legendary King Jim.

Upon returning to the ship, the First Mate took to his cabin for several days, where he remained in his bunk, afflicted by fever, and attended by his loyal harpooner, Mulongo. When at last Mr. Godward returned to the top decks, the crew was shocked to see his hair was now white as snow. Never an out-going soul to begin with, the taciturn New Bedford-man now only consorted with the crew when necessary, preferring to keep to himself, save for the company of the African who had saved his life.

One night I, along with a number of my shipmates, elected to sleep on the foredeck in hopes of enjoying the occasional breeze, as the fo'csle was as stifling as an oven in the heat of the equator. As I prepared to bed down, I spotted Mr. Godward standing at the rail, staring out at the darkness. His eyes shone in the moonlight, as if still wracked with fever. His lips were moving, although I heard no words, and, at first, thought that he was praying. Then I saw his mouth twist into a hateful grimace, and I realized that whatever the First Mate was doing, it had nothing to do with God.

One would think that after having this boat stove in and all hands drown, save for Mulongo, that Mr. Godward would be hesitant to return to the hunt. But nothing could be farther from the truth. As soon as he had regained his health, the First Mate picked a new crew to replace the one drowned and set forth in pursuit of whales in one of the extra boats stored on the boat-deck, with the ever-present Mulongo seated in the bow.

It was three months since we lost Haraldson when we first hove into view of the Marquesas, fifteen since we first set sail from Sag Harbor. Nuka Hiva was the largest of the eight islands that compose the archipelago, and although the French had recently laid claim to the island chain, Taiohae Bay had long been a popular destination for ships of all nations looking to take on supplies and refresh their weary crews.

The western side of the island consisted of imposing, rocky coasts, girdled by soaring cliffs, which occasionally broke to allow glimpses of deep coves that opened onto lush valleys, separated by towering spires cloaked in clouds and laced with waterfalls. The coastline to the east was equally difficult, with the trade wind generated waves pounding against the cliffs with earth-shaking reports. In contrast, the northern and southern sides of the island boasted several deep, sheltering bays that allowed easy access to the interior.

As the *Absolom* made its way between the towering twin islets that marked the entrance to the bay, we were greeted by the sight of a vast, horse-shoe shaped natural harbor, beyond which could be seen the island's lush vegetation, pierced by brooding volcanic pinnacles. After so long at sea, our arrival at Nuka Hiva was indeed a relief. The crew of the *Absolom* crowded the railings, our hungry senses thrown wide to receive the sights, sounds and scents of dry land. As we drew closer to the verdant shores, the breeze from the island carried with it the perfume of plumeria, jasmine and copra, all of which grew wild in the interior and in great abundance. For a boy raised on a Pennsylvania farm, it was the very breath of exotic paradise.

To the east of the bay was a stone wharf that dated back to when America kept a garrison on the island. Beyond it stood the canoe houses, and further still could be seen a small village. Scattered amongst the native huts fashioned from yellow bamboo with thatched roofs made of palmetto fronds were more conventional, European-style structures created by the French colonialists.

The moment *Absolom* dropped anchor, the villagers poured out of their huts and into the canoe house, dragging forth the massive outriggers South Sea Islanders are famous for. Since the Marquesas were very isolated, in relation to other islands in the Pacific, the natives were extremely quick to trade with passing ships. Within minutes the *Absolom* found itself surrounded on all sides by bobbing canoes filled with eager, shouting islanders touting everything from coconuts to live, trussed chickens waved about like living feather dusters.

One of the natives—a lovely young *wahine* with long, dark tresses and dressed in naught but a drape of linen about her waist—was so determined to sell her wares, she leapt from her canoe and began swimming in the direction of the ship's anchor chain. The sailors lined along the rail began to hoot and laugh, eagerly waving the girl onward.

Suddenly, I caught sight of a shadow in the water, moving swiftly towards the unwary swimmer. I felt a skeletal hand close about my heart as the dorsal fin broke the surface. *"Shark ho!"* I shouted, pointing to the deadly beast slicing its way through the waves.

As the crew of the *Absolom* scrambled for their harpoons

and firearms, I leapt onto the starboard rail, knife in hand, and was about to leap into the bay in a desperate attempt to save the girl from the monster's fearsome jaws, when a second, slighter shadow shot through the surf, striking the shark in its side, just below the gills. Stunned by the blow, the *mako* went rigid and promptly dropped like a stone to the bottom of the bay.

The second, silvery shadow then leapt free of the water in a jubilant pirouette, revealing itself to be a bottlenose dolphin. A mighty cheer rose from the crew as the porpoise continued to sport about the swimming girl, much like a sheepdog herding its charge into a paddock. Upon reaching the ship, the lovely native mermaid ignored the rope ladder that Marcus tossed over the side and, instead, chose to clamber up the anchor chain like a monkey climbing a tree.

As I hopped back down onto the deck, I found Captain Solomon watching me with a smile on his face. "By damn, when I saw you jump to the rail to try and save that girl, I thought I was back twenty-five years ago!" he said, puffing on his pipe. "You have your uncle's guts as well as blood in you, Padgett!"

"Thank you, sir. But I *didn't* save her," I said, gesturing to the girl, who now stood, still dripping from the sea, surrounded by eager, leering deckhands who had not seen a woman, white or otherwise, since liberty in Peru. She seemed in no way perturbed by the fact she had narrowly escaped being attacked by a shark, and, instead, was trying to interest the sailors gathered around her in the breadfruit she had brought with her in a bag made of netting. "The dolphin did."

"Aye, but you were ready to jump in between her and that toothy devil, which is more than any other man on this ship was willin' t'do, m'self included. And maybe if you had—and lived to tell the tale—you would have won yourself a wife in the bargain, just like your Uncle Cal did."

"Beg pardon, Cap'n?" I said, blinking in surprise.

"Ah, so he never told you about Amura did he?" Solomon sighed, tapping the bowl of his pipe against the rail as he dumped its ashes into the bay. "She was a lovely thing—barely tattooed, compared to most of 'em. She's the one that gave him that amulet," he said, gesturing to the dolphin pendant about my neck. "She was his wife whenever we were near Tahiti. She was carryin' his child when the mast snapped and took his legs. Cal refused to go back to her after that. Said he didn't want to be a burden, what with him bein' a cripple and all. I have no doubt she would have loved him all the same, legs or no legs, but your uncle had his pride."

"What happened to her and the child?" I asked, stunned to learn that not only did I have an aunt I never knew of, but a cousin as well.

Captain Solomon shrugged. "I suppose they're dead. After your uncle lost his legs, he gave me a packet of money and a letter to deliver to Amura the next time I was in Tahiti. Of course, it took me a year or more to get there. Once I arrived, I went to the hut she and Cal shared, which was built on the beach, only to find it long deserted. I asked around and discovered that when Cal didn't return that season, like he usually did, she took their baby son in her arms and walked into the ocean, never to be seen again."

Chapter Six

Heaving Down—I Am Given My Liberty—The Toad Hole—In The Company Of His Lordship— Cannibals At The Bar

The primary reason for the *Absolom* putting to port in Taiohae Bay was simple maintenance. Whalers set sail on long voyages anywhere from three to five years in length, assuming they're lucky on the hunt. During that time, repairs must be made by the crew if the vessel is to remain sea-worthy. That meant dropping anchor in a sheltered cove from time to time, safe from the constant churning of the sea, and heaving down the ship so that the crew could bream, scrape, tar, and sheath and copper the hull below the waterline.

Heaving down a whaling bark is an exacting and time-consuming enterprise. At its worst, it is exceedingly dangerous, grueling work and, at its very best, it is merely hazardous, arduous labor, but there is no avoiding it.

After conferring with the resident harbor pilot—a tall, lanky, sunburned fellow with an English accent—Captain Solomon brought the *Absolom* alongside the wharf with the leeward side facing the shore. The crew then began lightening the ship, carrying everything from barrels of oil and casks of hardtack to the Captain's chamber pot ashore via the gangplanks. Items too heavy to be carried by hand, such as the try-works, were tackled-rigged from the lower yardarms. By emptying *Absolom* of her contents, and leaving only enough ballast to maintain stable equilibrium while heeled, less strain was placed on the careening tackle set just below the crosstrees on the mizzen and foremasts.

While half the crew was ferrying everything not battened down onto the wharf, the other half was busily planking over the ports and covering them with tarred canvas, plug, caulk and pitch to make sure no water would enter the hull on the leeward side.

The ship's carpenter, a fellow named Hawley, and his apprentice, as well as Santo and myself, were then sent in to construct angled platforms in the hatchways that would serve as staging areas for the crew manning the pumps required to keep the ship clear of the water that managed to seep in while she was hove down. We were also tasked with building temporary bulkheads, fore and aft, and abreast either side of the keelson, extending from the ship's floor to the orlop deck, in order to prevent the remaining ballast from shifting too far to either side.

While we were busy making sure the leeward side of the ship remained watertight, our fellow crew members were sent aloft to dismantle the rigging, clearing all spars above the lower masts. The careening block and tackle on the fore and main masts was then attached to a capstan on the wharf, manned by nine strong men. As they pushed against the bars, the *Absolom* was pulled leeward via its masts, causing her to tip to one side and reveal her barnacle-encrusted hull.

Once careened, the job at hand began at a rapid pace, as the ship had to be returned to its natural position as soon as possible to avoid unnecessary strain on the hull and rigging. Strips of copper sheathing below the waterline that had been lost during our outward voyage were quickly replaced from the ship's stores, while sailors swarmed the exposed bottom like ants on a lump of sugar, vigorously scrubbing at the barnacles that clung to its underside with coconut shells, all the while dangling from Jacob's ladders secured from the upper railings. Meanwhile, another brace of hands cut away at the acres of trailing sea weed that had become tangled in the ship's keel and rudder.

Come dusk, the ship was righted to its natural position once more, so that the crew could be fed and bedded down in the foc'sle, in anticipation of repeating the exact same labors the very next day, until all the repairs that were needed were finished. As for the captain and his mates, they spent the evening in the villa of the *administrateur d'Etat*, enjoying his table and French wine, while the rest of the crew dined on hardtack, salt beef and cold coffee.

The *Absolom's* stores and cargo remained on shore, watched over by a brace of armed men, who were not there merely to guard the provisions from thieving locals, but to make sure none of the crew snuck off the ship in search of female companionship or escape their contracted servitude by fleeing to the interior of the island.

It says something as to the harshness and general unpleasantness of the average whaling man's s life that there were those on board who would gladly risk cannibal tribes rather than spend another season breathing smoke from the blubber-fires.

And so my first week in the tropical paradise of Nuka Hiva was spent scraping barnacles and sweetening the ship's bilge by pumping it dry and then rinsing it with pine oil. Every waking moment was spent at the hardest labor, under a broiling sun, yet I could not bring myself to grumble about my lot, for whenever I raised my eyes from the task at hand, I found myself staring at the most gorgeous landscape imaginable. I can honestly say I have never busted my back and raised blisters on my hands in lovelier surroundings.

Once everything was taken care of, and the *Absolom* was made as sound as possible under such circumstances, the vessel was righted for good and the cargo and equipage returned to their proper places within the holds. After everything was declared ship-shape by the bo'sun, the captain had the entire crew gather below the poop deck, from whence he addressed us.

"Laddies, you have done *Absolom* proud! I daresay she's as fit now as she was when she set sail from Sag Harbor! Mr. Godward and Mr. Gusset inform me that morale is so high that they only had to flog two or three of you. As reward for such diligence to the greater good, I am grantin' the starboard watch twenty-four hours liberty, startin' at two bells; then, once they've returned, the port watch gets its fun."

A loud huzzah arose from the gathered sailors upon hearing this news, with the starboard watch—of which I was a member—cheering the loudest.

"I warn you, though," Captain Solomon continued, shouting to make himself heard above the roar. "Keep to Taiohae, no matter what you do. And under no circumstances are you to go wanderin' off into the interior! I don't care how lovely the young lady may be or how many sisters she has at home—the valleys hereabout are thick with cannibals. And if the savages get their hands on you—well, even if you escape the cook pot, they're just as likely to mark you for life with heathen tattoos."

Having said his piece, the captain returned to his quarters and I and the others headed to the forecastle to set about adorning ourselves in what passed for our Sunday best, in hopes of attracting the favors of some pretty little *wahine*.

I doused myself in bay rum, as there was no means of bathing on board, tied a fresh kerchief about my neck and polished my dolphin amulet and arrayed it so that it was plainly visible against my shirt. At the sounding of two bells, I and the rest of the starboard watch hurried ashore across the gangplanks as if the hounds of hell were snapping at our heels.

Standing at the end of the wharf was a native covered in tattoos. He was nearly bent double from age, and the designs that crowded his withered body had faded from black to bluish-gray. As we approached, the picturesque Methuselah began reciting in a sing-song voice, alternating between French and English.

"Welcome travelers! *Bienvenue voyageurs!* Come to the Toad Hole! *Rendezvous au Trou Crapaud!* Best tavern in Taiohae! *Meilleure taverne à Taiohae!* Only tavern in Taiohae! *Seule taverne à Taiohae!*"

"Very well, grandfather!" Jones the Orkneyman laughed. "Take us to this wondrous 'Toad Hole' of yours!"

The old man grinned, revealing toothless gums, and motioned to Jones and the other to follow him. Moving with surprising alacrity, he lead the crocodile of laughing sailors past the huge canoe house that dominated the beach and into the grove behind it, until, a few minutes later, we emerged in a clearing, in the center of which was a structure that was a mixture of civilized and savage design. Although made of native bamboo, with a long, steeply peaked thatched roof similar to that found on the canoe house, it otherwise resembled a standard European dwelling and even included a wide verandah, the supporting posts of which were covered in carvings of the grimacing heathen gods known as *tiki*.

Standing in the shade of the porch was a short, squat flat-faced European with thinning hair and protruding eyes. He was dressed in a linen suit that may have, at one time, been white, but was now closer to ecru, with darker, tea-colored stains under his arm pits and around his collar. Upon seeing the group of eager sailors emerge from the tree line, he smiled and mopped his sweaty brow with an equally dingy handkerchief.

The old native hurried up to the man in the linen suit, speaking rapidly in his savage tongue, eagerly gesturing to the sailors he had brought. The European nodded and handed him a small flask of rum. The old man snatched the proffered liquor and hurried away, no doubt to consume his payment as fast as possible.

"Greetings, *mes amis!*" the Frenchman announced in a hoarse, croaking voice. "Welcome, men of the *Absolom* to my humble establishment! *Je suis Crapaud!* Whatever your heart desires can be had here, for a modest price. Is it cuisine you seek? *Mais bien sûr!* Drink? *Oui, oui!* Or perhaps you hunger for the company of *une jolie fille*, or *un beau garçon*? Crapaud holds the keys to the house of Venus, no matter which door you prefer!"

Upon entering, I saw that the interior of the tavern consisted of a single, barracks-like room, with tables and chairs fashioned from rattan and bamboo. Several beautiful young native girls, each lovelier than the last, and all of them nude from the waist up, were busy carrying platters of food and drink to the various customers. I stared, open-mouthed until it felt as if my eyes might grow stalks. Although the last fifteen months aboard the

Absolom had gone a long way to making me a man, I was still innocent as to the secrets of the fairer sex.

A *wahine* crossed the room and placed a small bundle of taro leaves bound with twine before a man dressed in the uniform of the French navy. The sailor took his knife and cut the string, and the leaves unfurled to reveal a succulent pork loin. Upon catching the scent of the roasted meat, I forgot all about the shameless naked flesh on display. After months spent living off jerked meat, hardtack and the thinnest of stews, the sight and smell of freshly prepared food was enough to make me drool like a starving hound.

"Jonas! Over here!"

I did not immediately respond to the shout, for I was still unaccustomed to my 'new' Christian name. I then spotted Santo seated at a table near the bar. The ship's cooper had been given his liberty far earlier in the day, and had gone into the village to barter with the trading post for a new blade for his saw. He must have succeeded in his quest, for he was now drinking rum in the company of the local harbor pilot.

"Come! Have a drink!" Santo's companion said with a laugh, motioning for me to join them. Despite his bare feet, sunburned complexion, and lack of a shirt, he spoke with an educated British accent and held his leather tankard like it was the finest cut crystal. "The name's John Michael Arthur Aubrey Monkeith III," he said, offering me his hand as I sat down. "But the locals call me Your Lordship to my face and His Lordship to everyone else."

"Jona—um, Jonas Padgett," I replied awkwardly. If His Lordship considered the fact I stumbled over my own name awkward, he had the breeding not to show it. "Are you really a lord?" I asked, eager to shift the conversation away from myself.

"Only if two brothers and three nephews die before I do," he laughed ruefully. "I'm what is known as a 'remittance man'. That is to say, my family pays me to stay away—and as *far* as possible. My father was *most* insistent on that last part, thanks to a series of unfortunate misunderstandings between myself a number of creditors in London.

"It might sound cruel on the behalf of the old *pater familias,* but to be honest, I don't miss England—the weather there is miserable—and I *certainly* don't miss my family—save for my mother, bless her. I was originally sent to the Caribbean to oversee the family's sugar plantation, but I ran afoul of yet *another* misunderstanding in Barbados, which necessitated my signing on with a whaler headed 'round the Horn. That's how I ended up on this beauteous island paradise—by jumping ship the first chance I got!

"Of course, back then Nuka Hiva was called Madison Island and was under the American flag. I stayed after your countrymen abandoned their outpost, and when the French staked their claim, they made me the harbor pilot since I know the waters hereabouts like I know the alphabet, the natives know me and like me well enough not to have eaten me yet, and I can speak their tongue as well as French. The colonial government pays me a little stipend for my services, and once a year the mail ship arrives with a packet from my elder brother, the new Earl—my father having succumbed to chronic high dudgeon some time ago—that allows me to keep myself properly amused during the monsoon seasons.

"I suspect, once my mother finally passes away, the remittance payments will cease altogether, but until that time, I am more than willing, and capable, of buying myself and anyone else, should it suit my fancy, a round of drinks. So what will it be, young Padgett?"

"If it's all the same to you, Your Lordship," I replied, wiping at the saliva at the corner of my mouth, "I would like to have something to eat."

"Of course! Poor boy, you must be famished! I remember all too well the filth they served aboard the whaler that brought me here." His Lordship snapped his fingers and one of topless bar maids suddenly appeared at our table like a *houri* summoned from heaven. "Petani, my dear, sweet girl," the Englishman said with a politely drunken smile, "please bring my young friend here the house special—and some more rum, while you're at it."

As I waited for my food to arrive, I took the occasion to study my surroundings a bit more closely. Most of the clientele seemed to be split between French colonists and the crew from the *Absolom*, but there were also a handful of natives mixed amongst them as well that were not acting as wait-staff. A pair of tribesmen sat cross-legged on woven mats set on the floor, talking amongst themselves as they drank from hand-carved bowls. Both men were as hairless as eggs, with shaved heads that gleamed like polished stone, and each wore necklaces fashioned from shark's teeth. Although their limbs were covered with intricate tattoos, their faces were unmarked, save for three long, curving dark lines inked onto the sides of their throats.

I also spotted a tall, powerfully built fellow, seated by himself at a nearby table, sipping grog from the shorn half-shell of a coconut. But where the other natives bore tattooing on their arms and legs, his were bare of adornment. Instead, his torso was covered in a design that resembled a great tidal wave eternally crashing in upon itself. Thrust through his ear-lobes were two small, intricately scrimshawed sperm-whale teeth, and a similar piece of ivory pierced his nose. In odd contrast to his barbarous appearance, he wore a watch-cap pulled down over his otherwise hairless head.

"That's an unusual piece you're wearing," His Lordship said, drawing my attention away from the naked savage in the wool cap. He gestured to the dolphin amulet hung about my neck. "Wherever did you find it?"

"It was left to me by my uncle," I explained. "It's my good luck charm." Before I could explain any farther, the wahine returned with a large wooden platter on which was arrayed a bowl of grayish-purple mash, a bundle of taro leaves wrapped in twine, and a bottle of rum. As my meal was placed before me, she flashed me a smile that almost made me forget the gnawing hunger in my belly.

"Don't worry about table manners, old chap," His Lordship laughed as I looked about for eating utensils. "The natives eat everything with their hands, including the *poi*." He demonstrated by plunging his first two fingers into the sticky substance and, with a practiced twirl, popped the purple-coated digits into his mouth.

I followed his example, although with considerably less expertise and far more mess. Still, despite my ineptitude, I managed to get enough of the poi into my mouth to find it sweet and starchy, and agreeable to the Western palate. I then eagerly tore open the taro leaf and began stuffing the tender morsels of roast pork into my mouth. After months of whaler's rations, I had to keep from swooning in ecstasy. As I hungrily gobbled down my meal, the Toad Hole's proprietor waddled up to the table.

"I trust you and your companions find everything *satisfaisant*, Your Lordship?" Crapaud asked as he mopped the back of his neck with his sodden handkerchief.

"Everything is *magnifique* as always, *mon ami*," His Lordship replied as he pulled the cork out of the rum bottle with his teeth.

Just then I looked up from my meal to see a third native join the pair seated on the floor. His loins were girt by heavy folds of *tapa*, hanging fore-and-aft in clusters of braided tassels, and his limbs were covered in elaborate tattooing that reminded me of my dear mother's lace patterns. But what truly caught my attention was the scar that traversed the right side of his face, and the fact his corresponding eye had been reduced to a withered, gray dead thing hiding in the back of its socket. From the way that his companions greeted him, it was obvious this man was their superior, possibly even a chieftain, although I could not spot any outward sign that differentiated him from the others, save the wound to his face.

As the one-eyed native moved to join his tribesmen, he glanced in the direction of our table and abruptly froze. He then fixed upon me a flat and unwavering stare with his remaining eye, regarding me with such harshness I instinctively recoiled. I was as much baffled as I was unnerved, for I could not ascertain what I could possibly have done to earn such a hostile glare. The native then said something to one of his companions, nodding in my direction as he did so. As the tribesmen spoke amongst themselves, I was alarmed to discover that their teeth were as sharp as those strung around their necks.

Seeing the look on my face, His Lordship gave an amused laugh. "So you've finally noticed the cannibals at the bar, have you?"

I turned to stare at Crapaud in disbelief. "You allow such

beings in your place of business?" I gasped.

The Frenchman shrugged his shoulders. *"Monsieur,* if I was to bar all those who have tasted human flesh from my establishment, I would be out of business in a week! All natives on this island, and the others that surround it, partake in the ritual of the cannibal at one time or another in their lives."

"That is true," Santo agreed with a sage nod of his head. "But there are tribes considered cannibals even amongst the cannibals."

"You mean the Typee," His Lordship said darkly.

"Is that what those three gentlemen are?" I asked nervously.

"Non," Crapaud replied with a shake of his head. "The Typee, they keep to their valley. I do not know what tribe these claim, but they are not of Nuka Hiva. Perhaps they hail from Tahuata or Eiao?" The Frenchman turned to address the harbor pilot, who was busy pouring another finger or two of rum into his tankard. "What do you think, Your Lordship? You know the Marquesans far better than I do."

His Lordship set aside his bottle and contemplated the trio of savages like an ornithologist attempting to identify a species of bird. "Whatever they are, they aren't Marquesans. I do not recognize their tattoos as belonging to the tribes on this or any of the islands in the chain."

"You mean you can tell all that by the scribble on their bodies?" I exclaimed in surprise.

"It may look like meaningless scrawl to you, my young friend—but it is much, much more. In a world where everyone walks around starkers, there's still got to be a way to show that you're a high *muckamuck,* or what's the point of being one? And I say that, coming from a long line of *muckamucks,* myself. No, the tattoos on a native tell you who they are, what their tribe is, and their role and importance within it. And each tribe has a style and set of designs unique to itself. I've lived on Nuka Hiva for twelve years, and I have never seen those markings before."

Suddenly the trio of cannibals got to their feet and left, but not before the one-eyed leader threw me a venomous parting glare.

"It would seem their head-man does not care for the cut of

your jib," His Lordship commented drily.

"But how could I have possibly insulted him? I didn't even speak to him!" I exclaimed.

"Who knows what goes on in the mind of a savage?" the Englishman replied with a shrug. "I have known them to take offense at the slightest provocation. Perhaps they believe you have broken a tabu of their tribe? Not that it matters. Your ship sets sail in a day or two, does it not? So bugger the cannibal bastards and have another drink."

I spent the rest of the day drinking rum and swapping stories with His Lordship and Santo, growing increasingly inebriated as afternoon stretched into dusk then lengthened into evening. Upon seeing both Santo and me stifle a yawn, our newly found friend suggested that we should spend the night at his bungalow. I found the idea of sleeping somewhere besides the fetid confines of the foc'sle quite appealing, and had no trouble in coercing Santo into accompanying me.

After settling our tab, the three of us staggered out of the Toad Hole. His Lordship lead the way, armed with a torch provided by the ever-considerate Crapaud, while Santo and I followed close behind, arms linked about one another in the name of comradeship and mutual stability. Thus armed against the night, and whatever dwelt within it, we headed in the direction of the beach.

Chapter Seven

His Lordship's Estate—Santo's Family—Strange Sounds In The Night—The Nightmare Island—Awakened By Cannibals

His Lordship lived in a bungalow cottage located on the wide, horseshoe-shaped beach, less than ten minutes' walk from the wharf where the *Absolom* was anchored. It was built of bamboo and had a thatched roof and sat upon a stone foundation, and boasted a wide porch supported by heavy wooden posts.

"Welcome to my estate," His Lordship said with a drunken laugh. "It's not much, compared to what my brother inherited, but I daresay the climate and view are a damn sight better." He gestured to the vast, natural amphitheater of the bay, barely a hundred feet from his doorstep. He quickly ducked inside the one-room cottage and returned with a straw-wrapped jug. "I try to keep a little palm wine on hand, should I have visitors," he explained with a laugh. The exiled aristocrat sloshed the milky liquid into a trio of empty tins that had once contained corned beef, but now served as drinkware.

I gave the stuff a wary sniff before trying it, but the moment I tasted its sweetness on my tongue, I tilted the can back and drained it dry. It tasted like very sweet jelly coconut water, with just a touch of vinegar, and I quickly decided I quite liked it.

"Be careful, boy," Santo laughed knowingly. "Palm wine, she is sweet, but she is strong—like my wife!"

"I didn't know you were married, Santo," I said in surprise. Although we had worked side-by-side for months, the cooper and I rarely had time for small talk as we were too busy creating casks and barrels to do more than talk shop.

"*Sim,*" he said, with a proud smile. "She is *muito bonita,* my Madalena. I go to sea *quatro, cinco anos,* yes? Then I return to my village of Nazaré with my pay. I spend a year with my family. Then I go back to sea. Every time I leave, my wife, she is big in the belly. I have *cinco filhos*: Branco, Gomes, Salazar and Renata."

"That's only four," His Lordship pointed out as he sipped his palm wine.

"Like I said, my Madalena, she big when I go. When I next return to Nazaré, I see if she has son or daughter for me."

"Your wife doesn't mind you being away from home for so long?" I asked.

"*Não!*" the cooper said with a laugh. "We are husband and wife twenty *anos.*" He held his right hand, splaying the fingers. "But we only live together *cinco anos.* Every time I return, we are like new, yes?" he said with a wink.

"Doesn't your *senhora* worry that you will be unfaithful while you're away?" His Lordship queried.

"My Madalena, she know I never betray her with another woman," Santo replied with a solemn shake of his head. "All this time, I never touch another *garota*—not even a *wahine* or *prostituta.*

"Most commendable," His Lordship said with a crooked smile as he sloshed another round of palm wine into our waiting tins. "I propose a toast to your matrimonial fortitude in the face of temptation!"

I eagerly downed another draught, and then another. But I soon discovered what Santo had said about the drink's potency was indeed true. I found myself too drunk to stand, much less crawl into one of the hammocks His Lordship had kindly strung up on the his porch for us to use, and ended up passing out on a tapa mat, which proved no harder than my regular berth aboard the *Absolom.*

I woke up about an hour later, still drunk and more than a little disoriented. I looked out toward the beach and saw that the moon and stars above the bay had moved in the night sky. I wondered to myself what could have roused me from my sodden slumber. I glanced in the direction of Santo's hammock, only to find my shipmate nowhere to be seen.

It was then I heard a low, muffled sound, like that of someone groaning in pain. As I struggled to push the fog from my mind, I recognized the voice as belonging to Santo, and that the sound seemed to be coming from inside the cottage. I got up from my palette and peered through the window, which was covered by a thin curtain of mosquito netting.

Santo stood with his back to me, his pants down about his ankles, revealing his muscular, hairy legs. His head was angled as if he was studying the thatching of the roof, and his hands were firmly planted on his hips, which rocked slightly to and fro. His Lordship knelt before the cooper, his head bobbing up and down rapidly. Whatever Santo was feeling, it most certainly wasn't pain. While I was surprised to see my shipmate in such a compromising position, I was far from shocked. One does not spend fifteen months in the fo'csle without becoming familiar with what lonely men do in the dark when they think no one else is awake.

Seeing that my friend was not in any danger, I discretely returned to my makeshift bed, leaving Santo to remain faithful to his wife, in his fashion.

As I lay back down, I turned my drowsy eyes in the direction of the nearby beach and listened to the sound of the surf, which filled my ears like the breathing of a giant, until it lulled me back to sleep.

"Row, you dogs!"

I was in the whale boat, pulling on the oars. I did not know how I had come to be there, nor did I remember anything leading up to that moment. Instead, it was as if I had spontaneously generated between the gunwales. I looked about and saw we were in the middle of the ocean, and that the *Absolom* was nowhere in sight.

Captain Solomon sat at the tiller, his pipe clenched between his teeth, his solitary eye fixed on the horizon beyond my straining back. As my gaze fell upon the others in the boat, I was surprised to find Haraldson amongst their number, his beard and mustaches decorated with strands of seaweed.

"Put your backs into it, laddies!" the captain shouted urgently. "We have to make that island before the storm o'er takes us!"

Upon hearing the words 'island' and 'storm', I paused in my rowing to glance behind me, and saw, in the near distance, a dark mass rising above the waterline, and, in the farther distance, a rapidly approaching squall line, its thick, black thunderheads laced with lightning. My heart leapt in terror at the thought of being caught on the open water in such conditions, and I resumed my efforts in double-time.

It was not long before we reached what Captain Solomon had called, rather optimistically, an island. In truth, it was more a barren hummock of rock. It looked to me like the uppermost portion of an underwater mountain thrust skyward by some recent volcanic upheaval on the ocean floor. As there was no beach-head in evidence, the captain ordered us to maneuver as close as possible, so that Haraldson could leap onto its sloping shore.

Once there, the Swede was thrown the whale-line and then each of us, in turn, shinnied across like rats onto a ship. Once all of us were on the shore of the strange island, we heaved as one on the line, pulling the boat up after us. Once it was safely ashore, only then was I free to turn my attention to our surroundings.

The island looked to be no more than a mile long, and half as wide, like a great loaf of bread afloat in the middle of the Pacific. The ground was black as a bible and reeked strongly of fish. There was no vegetation anywhere to seen on its godforsaken expanse, nor were there any rock formations.

"He's near," Captain Solomon said, taking the pipe from his mouth and tilting his head back to stare at the broiling sun tacked high in the sky. "I can feel him."

"Who do you mean, Cap'n?" I asked.

"King Jim, of course," he replied. "Or did you forget what we've been chasin' all this time?" With that he bit back down on the pipe stem and began trudging towards the center of the tiny island, Haraldson and the others trailing after him.

As I hurried after my shipmates, the toe of my boot struck against something, nearly causing me to fall on my face. I bent down to investigate and saw a twisted length of metal, about the length and breadth of my hand jutting from the otherwise smooth surface of the islet. I tugged on it and, to my surprise, pulled it free like Arthur drawing Excalibur from the stone. But instead of a sword, what I held in my hand was a harpoon.

As I did so, the ground beneath me began to tremble and roil, like the skin of a horse seeking to rid itself of flies. Captain Solomon and the others were knocked down like a set of duckpins by the earthquake. There then came a rumbling sound, from deep within the island itself, and suddenly a geyser burst forth not far from where I stood, showering me in bright red gore.

As I staggered backward, wiping at the blood streaming down into my face, I saw Captain Solomon, the dead Swede and the others lose their purchase in the scarlet downpour and slide off the back of the awakened sea-beast and plunge into the ocean below. I watched in horror as my captain and fellow shipmates were torn limb from limb before my eyes by the monstrous sharks that filled the churning waters.

Suddenly there came a noise unlike any I had ever heard before, louder than any roar voiced by mortal throat. I cried out in horror and clamped my hands to my ears, for no man can hear the call of the ocean god and survive unscathed.

I awoke to the sound of Santo cursing in his native tongue. As I opened my eyes, I was greeted by the sight of the Portugee trapped within his hammock, flanked on either side by the cannibals I had seen earlier at the Toad Hole.

The one-eyed headman stepped forward while the others pinned the cooper's arms to his sides, keeping him from rolling free, and bared his horrible filed teeth. The cannibal's mouth seemed to grow to hideous proportions, like a snake unhinging its jaw, before he bit deep into Santo's exposed belly. The cooper's angry shouts quickly dissolved into shrieking, the likes of which I had never heard from a human being.

As I lay there in the shadows, paralyzed with horror, the

one-eyed cannibal yanked free a length of my friend's guts, causing them to unravel from his torso like a magician's scarf. The savage then swallowed the mouthful of pulsing, living flesh whole, without the use of his hands, his throat seeming to expand as he gulped down his hideous meal.

Excited by my the smell of their victim's blood and the sight of his agonized thrashing, the remaining cannibals set upon poor, doomed Santo, ripping into his struggling body like a pair of boars rooting for truffles.

"Get off my porch, you bloody bastards!" His Lordship yelled as he charged out of the bungalow, armed with a native paddle-spear fashioned of *koa* wood. The Englishman attempted to brain the one-eyed cannibal with the oar blade, but his opponent proved far too swift. The savage dodged the blow while sweeping the aristocrat's legs out from under him, causing His Lordship to drop the weapon. The cannibal headman snatched up the paddle-spear and drove its business-end through His Lordship's chest, pinning him like a butterfly.

The sight of the blood spurting from the dying man's mouth, like the crimson geyser in my nightmare, shocked me from my paralysis. Leaping to my feet, I ran towards the beach and the direction of the *Absolom*.

As I sped across the sandy beach, I heard angry shouts behind me. I glanced over my shoulder and instantly wished I had not looked. The trio of cannibals were in close pursuit, their tattooed faces smeared with the blood of my friends, their horrible, shark-like maws opened impossibly wide, as if to swallow me whole.

Part Three
The Whale Rider

Chapter Eight

A Unexpected Savior—Koro—I Become Ship's Cooper—
The New Harpooner—The Watchers On The Hill

Ifled my dreadful pursuers as fast as I could, my heart climbing my ribs like a ladder until I feared it would escape into
my throat. I did not dare cast a second look behind me, for fear
the sight would unman me completely. Separated from my
shipmates aboard the *Absolom*, I was on my own against the
dreadful trio of bloodthirsty murderers chasing me like a pack
hounds going after a rabbit.

Suddenly a dark shape stepped out from the palm trees that
lined the shore, looming before me like one of the natives' stone
gods. I cried out in alarm, thinking one of the cannibals had
outflanked me. However, to my complete surprise, the shadowy
figure pushed me aside and hurled what looked to be a spear at
the killers behind me.

The savage at the head of the pack gave a single shriek of
agony and dropped to the sand like a pole-axed steer, the haft
of a harpoon jutting from his chest. His companions halted to
stare down at their slain tribesman. The one-eyed headman
then looked up and said something angrily in his heathen
tongue, loudly slapping his naked chest with a splayed hand.

In response, my unexpected savior took a step forward into
the moonlight, pulling a knife from the hand-woven belt about
his waist. It was then I recognized him as the solitary native
I had seen at the Toad Hole earlier that evening, the one with
the watch cap. He answered the cannibal with his own stream
of heated gibberish, all while making menacing gestures with

his blade. Whatever he said must have proved persuasive, for the remaining cannibals abruptly turned on their heels and fled toward the bay.

As I watched in amazement, the tribesmen leapt head-first into the surf and disappeared, leaving their dead comrade behind on the beach. They were either very strong swimmers or drowned almost immediately, for I saw no more sign of them. It was as if the water had swallowed them alive.

The native who had rescued me grunted in disgust and strode over to the body of the man he'd just killed. From the casual manner in which he yanked free the harpoon, you would have thought he had just brought down a wild boar as opposed to a fellow human.

"Thank you, my friend, for delivering me from those horrid cannibals!" I exclaimed, offering him my hand. "My name is Padgett. Jo—uh, Jonas Padgett. What is you name, good sir?"

"I am called Koro of the Aina," the native replied, in surprisingly passable English. After a moment's hesitation he took my hand and shook it in a firm but friendly manner. The native was naked save for his loincloth, watch-cap, and the ink that covered his torso, and although a veritable giant, with muscles like pythons, seemed possessed of a genial and trustworthy nature.

"I do not know what brought you to this stretch of beach, Koro, but I am glad of it! I owe you my life, my friend!"

"I was hunting the Mano Kanaka," he said, pointing to the dead cannibal at his feet. "They are the ancestral enemy of my people, and I know their ways. I saw them follow you when you left. I knew they would try and kill you."

"If they were looking for a cannibal feast, why choose the three of us when there are plenty of solitary sailors wandering about tonight?"

Koro pointed to the dolphin talisman about my neck. "*That* is why the Mano Kanaka chose you. It is the totem of my people. That is what made them want to kill you, and it is what made me help you."

"My Uncle Calvin, rest his soul, always said this was a good luck charm," I said, patting the amulet like a faithful pet. "I must go now and alert the Captain as to what has happened. I would very much appreciate your company on these errands, friend Koro, in case those fiendish Mano Kanaka, as you call them, decide to come back."

"Whatever you wish of me, it is my honor to obey," the native said, bowing his head in acquiescence.

And that is how the greatest friendship of my life began.

Upon reaching the *Absolom*, I promptly reported to Mr. Levant, who was in charge of the night watch. I related how Santo and I had availed ourselves of His Lordship's generosity—although I left out the part about Santo availing himself of our host's hospitality even further—and the subsequent cannibal attack. By the time I'd gotten to my rescue by Koro, the Third Mate raised his bushy brows and proclaimed: "There's nothing much I would rouse the Cap'n for, save a typhoon or King Jim. But, by damn, I'm waking him up for this."

A few minutes later a bedraggled Captain Solomon emerged from his cabin with a sour look on his face. But upon seeing the harpoon-wielding Koro, dressed in his loincloth and watch-cap, his demeanor quickly changed. I once more related my story, and as I described the cannibals, I saw a glimmer of recognition in his eyes.

"Mano Kanaka, you say?" he muttered, rubbing his chin. "The tribe sounds familiar. I believe your uncle and I had a run in with such heathen man-eaters, long years ago, young Padgett. Very disagreeable buggers, if memory serves. Mr. Levant! Grab a lantern and gather a shore party! We've a fallen shipmate to claim."

The shore party sent to gather up what remained of Santo consisted of Captain Solomon, Mr. Levant, Koro, two deckhands, and me. The hands carried between them a roll of sailcloth plus needle and thread, and the rest of us bore lanterns to light our way. Just to be on the safe side, every one of us was also armed with a weapon, whether it was pistol, knife, hand-ax or belaying pin; while Koro, easily the most physically intimidating member of the expedition, carried his harpoon balanced on his shoulder like a soldier on parade.

As we re-traced our route along the beach, Captain Solomon called a halt upon spotting the body of the dead cannibal. "What a dreadful thing to be a man's last sight," he muttered as he examined the carcass. He frowned and pointed to the markings on either side of the dead man's neck. "What manner of wounds are those?"

AAs I stared down at the corpse, I realized that what I had initially mistaken for tattoos on either side of the cannibal's throat were, in fact, incisions of some sort, designed to resemble the gills of a fish.

"No doubt it's some type of heathen adornment, Cap'n," Mr. Levant suggested. "They're always muckin' with their bodies to make themselves look fierce to their enemies. That would explain their jaws as well." He nudged the cannibal's unusually wide mouth with its mouth full of jagged teeth. "I hear tell of African savages that stick plates in their lips and Red Indians that wrap their babies' heads to make the skull come to a point. There's no tellin' what fancy will take root in a primitive mind."

Captain Solomon's demeanor grew even grimmer once we reached the bungalow and what was left of Santo and His Lordship. "A harpoon to the heart is too good for the murderin' savages," he growled. "Get to work, maties—stitch up a proper sailor's shroud for the Portugee." He then nodded in my direction. "As for you, young Padgett—you're now the ship's cooper. I'll have your shares adjusted accordingly in the company books."

Normally I would have been pleased by such news, but given the conditions under which I found myself being elevated, I could take no joy in it. Santo had been a good fellow, and an excellent craftsman, one I would be hard-pressed to surpass. I thought about his beloved Magdalena, back in Portugal, now awaiting her husband's return from the sea in vain, and my heart grew heavier still.

Once Santo's body was sewn inside his canvas shroud, Captain Solomon ordered Mr. Levant and his men to stand guard over the corpses, in case the cannibals came back to finish their meal. He then had Koro and me escort him into the village, so we could repeat our story, yet again, to the French authorities.

The Governor's mansion was a two-story colonial-style edifice, similar to those found in Fiji, with wide verandas and shady porches built to shelter far-flung citizens of France from the punishing tropical sun. It was far from a palace, but compared to the humble huts of the surrounding natives, it was a veritable Versailles. As for the Governor himself, he was not in the least pleased at being dragged from his bed at such an hour, and unafraid to say so in every language he knew. But upon hearing my story, he lost no time in sending a squadron of soldiers from the nearby garrison to relieve Mr. Levant's watch and claim His Lordship's body.

It was dawn by the time I returned to the *Absolom*. Upon reaching the boarding plank, Captain Solomon stopped and turned to eye Koro, who had followed me, as silent and docile as a hound, every step of the way.

"I'm in sore need of a new harpooner, Koro. And I don't have to ask if you can throw that thing," he said. "The question is, are ye interested in signin' on?" "The question is, are ye interested in signin' on?"

Koro turned to look at me. "Will you be on the ship?" I nodded my head. He turned back to Captain Solomon and smiled. "Yes. I will be your new harpooner."

We buried Santo later that same day, along with His Lordship, as the tropic heat is not kind to corpses, especially ones so roughly treated. The cooper's final resting place was on a hillside with a splendid view of the bay. The ship's carpenter and I built a coffin from the lumber used to make the barrels and casks, in tribute to our fallen shipmate.

There was a decent turn out as Santo had been well-liked amongst the crew, and Captain Solomon recited a Psalm or two, since there were no missionaries on the island. His Lordship's mourners numbered only the Governor and Crapaud, who seemed genuinely grieved over the loss of his best customer. I wondered how many years the long-suffering brother back in England would continue sending remittance payments before discovering the family's black sheep was dead.

Once all was said and done, we trooped back to the *Absolom*, now re-provisioned and ready to set sail. As we left the island, I went to the rail to bid farewell to its wild, exotic beauty. As I looked toward the mountain spires, I espied two figures standing side-by-side on a grassy, wind-swept hill, watching the *Absolom* slip its way between Nuka Hiva's guardian islets. I rubbed my eyes and looked again, but all there was to see were a pair of freshly turned graves.

Chapter Nine

Freed From the Fo'c'sle—Reading The Waves—A Holiday Feast—Ghost Stories Before The Mast—A Christmas Swim

Upon being named ship's cooper there was not only an increase in my lay, but an upgrade in my accommodations aboard the *Absolom*. No longer was I consigned to the fo'c'sle, with its trapped farts and piss-soaked corners. Instead, I was to bunk in steerage, with the harpooners and other skilled members of the crew, such as the harpooners, blacksmith, carpenter and cook. My new digs were entered through the after hatch, located just forward of the main cabin and officers' quarters. On the port side were the bunk rooms, each of which held two sets of narrow bunk-beds, fitted with thin mattresses and even flatter pillows. After spending months sleeping on a bare wooden bunk, surrounded by twenty-three other men, it all seemed like the height of luxury.

Another perk of my new station was a much appreciated change in diet. Where before I had been forced to take my meals on the deck, I now dined in the main cabin, after the captain and the mates had left the table. And where once there was naught but hardtack, jerked beef, beans and cold coffee, now I feasted on fresh meats and fresh-made biscuits. Save for the lack of butter and sugar, and having to use molasses to sweeten my coffee, I daresay I ate as well as Captain Solomon himself!

As was to be expected, I took over Santo's berth and Koro claimed what had once been Haraldson's. And as luck would so have it, both happened to be in the same room. My other bunk-mates were the ship's carpenter, Hawley, and the blacksmith,

Cuppy, who were my elders by several years. While they proved genial enough living companions, it was clear that they viewed me with the same bemusement old dogs hold for a bumbling puppy. So it was only natural that I would gravitate more towards Koro's company during my off-hours.

There is a distinct social hierarchy onboard a whaling ship, and the harpooners are often viewed as a breed apart. Although the late Swede had proven affable enough, the majority kept to themselves and often took their mess seated together in the main cabin. Before my most singular introduction to Koro, I had never spoken more than a handful of words to any of the ship's harpooners, and I had most certainly never known a South Seas Islander before. Koro would prove my introduction to both worlds.

Upon signing on, Koro forsook his native loin cloth in favor of a pair of canvas pants, the cuffs of which halted a good inch or three above his ankles. Out of curiosity, he tried on one of the denim shirts in the Swede's sea chest, only to have it burst at the seams the first time he flexed his biceps. As he could not find a shirt to accommodate him, Koro decided to go about bare-chested, save for the swirls of ink that decorated his midriff. The only item of clothing he retained from our first meeting was the wool watch-cap, which he wore, day and night, atop his otherwise hairless head. He even wore it in his sleep.

As was to be expected, Koro's physical prowess made him a worthy addition to the crew. He was a tireless oarsman, whether in pursuit or the hauling-back, and would take his place between the gunnels without complaint. But what amazed me was his ability to read waves.

All mariners, in time, learn how to read the ocean by studying the stars and watching the clouds and birds. But in Koro's case, he could rest his hand atop the surface of the sea and divine from its movements how close land might be, and in which direction.

You might think that is so much sun-addled balderdash, but I assure you it is the truth. A stone thrown in a pond results in ripples, does it not? Any object that breaks the surface will affect the pattern of the ripples, whether the body of water is as small as a pond or as vast as the Pacific Ocean. Islands and atolls have the same effect as rocks. When waves hit an island, some are reflected back in the direction from which they came, while others are deflected at angles around the island and continue onward in a different form. The Polynesians are schooled in such navigation from birth, and that is how they can travel from Fiji to Tahiti without use of compass, maps, or sextants.

Simply by using his sense of touch, Koro was able to read the ripples and waves of the ocean the same way a phrenologist reads the bumps on one's head. This also held true for passing ships and the great beasts that we hunted, all of which he claimed generated their own unique patterns.

But as far as the *Absolom* was concerned, Koro's true worth lay in his skill with the harpoon, and in that there was no equal. If he threw an iron, it was certain to find its mark, and sink deep on first strike. He could all but thread the eye of a needle with the damned thing. There was no hauling back of lost throws whenever Koro stood in the bow, and I never once saw him flinch as the behemoths breached the surface, sending spray and spume in all directions. He always stood fast, as motionless as a statue, no matter how rough the seas.

Captain Solomon was very pleased with his new hire, and sang his praises every chance he got. This did not sit well with the other harpooners, of course, all of whom had been there far longer and considered themselves far more experienced in the business of whaling. However, if Koro was aware of the jealous looks cast his way by Mulogo and the others, he did not show it to me or anyone else.

On those evenings we were both at leisure, Koro and I would sit on the deck and watch the stars as they pinwheeled overhead. I would smoke my pipe while Koro covered a whale's tooth in scrimshaw and we would talk about the worlds we had left behind or the worlds we hoped one day to see. Although, in retrospect, I admit it was I who did most of the talking, while Koro did most of the listening. Still, those were good times, the kind you tuck away for colder, darker days, to remind yourself that there was time in your life where, for once, you were content with the world, and your place in it.

Of course, it could not last.

Normally, the life of a whaling man is one of deprivation and hard work that most outside the poor house will never know. However, there are two days of the year where the entire crew is allowed rest and pleasure. The first is the day commemorating the birth of our great country; the second is the day commemorating the birth of our blessed Savior.

In truth, the festivities aboard the *Absolom* began on Christmas Eve, with Pedro the cook preparing a proper holiday feast in the galley. Captain Solomon and his mates were presented with a roast suckling pig, with mashed potatoes and baked turnips, along with bottles of wine, while the skilled hands dined on boiled turkey with oyster sauce, washed down with sweet cider. As for the rest of the crew, in place of their usual meal of hardtack and jerked beef, there was a savory stew, and each hand was presented with a small mince pie and extra rations of rum.

While not all the hands aboard the *Absolom* were Christian—indeed, more than a few were heathens in the truest sense of the word—this did not deter them from sharing in the celebration. Jones the Orkneyman brought out his concertina and played a fine shanty, while Virgil, Homer, Marcus and Mulogo demonstrated the dances of their shared ancestry.

"Why do you rejoice tonight?" Koro asked, frowning in puzzlement as he watched the gathered crew sing and laugh and lift their leather flagons in merry toast.

"We're celebrating the birth of our god," I explained.

"A god has been born on our ship?" Koro exclaimed, looking about in surprise.

"No, my friend," I laughed, clapping him on one broad shoulder. "Our god was born long ago, in a land far away. He died but came back to us, and promises eternity in paradise if we give our love to Him and live by His rules. Tonight we honor His birth and the brotherhood of man, for through His love, all of us are as brothers for we are all His children."

"That is a good thing to celebrate," Koro conceded. "My people also honor our god, Tangaroa, Lord of the Ocean, with celebration."

Fearing I was about to hear a story of how hapless virgins are hurled alive into volcanoes to appease native gods, and thereby ruining my Christmas cheer, I cut Koro short by pouring him some more rum and stuffing a mince pie in his hand, both of which he eagerly consumed.

As the evening progressed and the merry-making continued, the conversation turned, as it always does on Christmas Eve, to the telling of ghost stories.

"Anyone ever hear tell of the *Caleuche*?" Cuppy the blacksmith asked.

"Ain't she a ghost ship what sails near Chiloe Island, off the coast of Chile?" Mr. Shreve, replied.

"Aye," the blacksmith said as he lit his pipe. "And a wondrous sight she is, shinin' beautiful and bright in the night, like a star on the water."

"How do you know *that*, Cuppy?" The second mate asked with a disbelieving laugh.

"Because I seen her with me own eyes, sir," the old man replied, tapping his right temple with the stem of his pipe. "It was long years ago, back when I shipped on the *Bunker Hill*. It was midnight and we was off the coast of the archipelago when I seen it. The whole ship were aglow, as if painted in Saint Elmo's Fire! And although I could hear the sounds of people laughin' and playin' music, like they was havin' themselves a fine party, there was no one to be seen on deck!

"Then, just as sudden as she appeared, the ship began to submerge—but not like she run aground. It was more like the soundin' of a whale, once they've taken their air. I looked down and I could see the ghost-ship glowin' under the water, sailin' beneath the waves as pretty as the *Bunker Hill* sailed on 'em! And as I watched, I seen a woman leave the captain's quarters and stand on the poop deck. Her body were human on one side, and fish on the other. The side that were human was beautiful beyond compare, with long blonde hair that floated about her head like a cloud. On the side that were fish, she was covered in golden scales."

"What you saw was the *Sirena Chilota*," Mr. Gussett said sagely. "She's a water spirit what escorts the souls of drowned sailors to the afterlife aboard the *Caleuche*. Once the dead are on board, they resume their lives as they were before they died."

"What he saw was the bottom of a bottle of rum, more like!" Mr. Shreve said with a dismissive laugh. "There ain't no such animal as a mermaid! I don't care what you call 'em, or what half of them be fishy and what half be woman!"

"I wouldn't be so quick to scoff, sir," Cuppy replied dourly. "I been on the water longer than most of you been alive. There's things in the ocean that no man can explain. Who is to say mermaids ain't one of them?"

"Not *all* merfolk got the nethers of a fish," Jones the Orkney man pointed out. "The selkie that haunt the waters of me people wear the skins of seals, they do. On Midsummer's Eve they come out of the sea and cast aside their selkie-skins and appear as beautiful women and handsome men. They dance on lonely stretches of beach, and bask in the sun on outlyin' skerries, for they have no human shame. Some even fall in love with mortal men and women, and have children with 'em—but in time, they all return to the sea. It's in their nature, y'know."

"Kamoho, King Of All The Sharks, often takes human lovers," Koro said suddenly, speaking in all earnestness. "When he crawls out of the sea to walk amongst the people of the land, he takes on the form of a mighty chief. Dressed in his majestic skin, he walks amongst them, partaking in their sports and enjoying their bounty, always looking for the most beautiful woman of the tribe. Once he finds her, he lies down with her and fills her belly with his seed, then returns to the sea."

"Sounds t'me like ol' Kamoho is a sailor," Mr. Shreve said with a wink and a nod.

"When it is the woman's time to deliver," Koro continued, ignoring the Second Mate's interruption, "she gives birth to a shark pup, not a human baby. Once she sees what she has brought forth, she hurls it into the sea, where it swims off in search of its father and its many brothers. When Kamoho's sons grow to adulthood, they, too, leave the ocean in the form of men to search for women and to feast on human flesh. They are the Mano Kanaka: the Eaters of Men; the Children of the Shark-God."

"The Mano Kanaka; isn't that the name of the cannibal tribe

that killed Santo?" I asked.

Koro nodded his head. "Yes. They are one and the same. One day a princess of my people was swimming in the bay when a Mano Kanaka saw her. The princess was very beautiful, but because the Mano Kanaka was in the water, he did not want to mate with her, but, instead, wanted to devour her. The princess swam very fast and very hard, but the Mano Kanaka swam even faster. Just when it seemed she could not escape, a sailor on a ship anchored in the bay leapt into the water and onto the back of the Mano Kanaka, stabbing it with his knife and killing it. The princess was so grateful to the brave sailor she became his wife."

"Them native girls, they know how to thank a man proper!" Mr. Shreve said with an inebriated guffaw. "Am I right, mates? None of that hand-holdin' in the front parlor with a pair of maiden aunties watchin' you like hawks! They know what a man needs from a woman, and ain't shy about givin' it to 'em! Why, I remember this little *wahine* in Fiji—breasts like peaches she had, and a bottom as firm as a melon..."

Koro's face flushed bright red and he abruptly got to his feet, leaving the Second Mate to regale his eager listeners about the pleasures of his Fiji conquest. The harpooner stalked over to the railing and stared down at the wine-dark ocean. I trailed after him, surprised by the sudden change in his normally good-natured mood.

"That story you told about the princess and the shark—that was just a legend, wasn't it?" I asked. "Like Jones' seal-people and Cuppy's ghost-ship?"

"No; it is a true story," he replied, not taking his eyes from the dark water. "It is the story of how I came into the world. The princess was my mother, and the sailor was my father."

I stood there for a long moment, thinking about Koro's tale and the story Captain Solomon had told me about how my Uncle Calvin once saved a native girl from a shark. Was it possible that Koro's father and Uncle Cal were the same man? It would certainly explain the strong sense of kinship I had felt towards him from the moment we first met. But such a thing was impossible. Captain Solomon said that Uncle Cal's bride had killed both herself and their son by walking into the sea.

I glanced down and saw that I was clutching the amulet my uncle had given me without realizing it. Perhaps it was the extra rations of rum, but for the tiniest moment the red coral dolphin almost seemed to stir within my hand.

After thoroughly partaking of the holiday's good spirits, I stumbled off to my bunk, leaving my fellow shipmates to continue their merry-making without me. I slept so soundly I barely registered the arrival of my bunk-mates when they finally trooped in, later in the evening.

A few hours later I found myself prodded awake by my bladder. I crawled out of my bunk and lifted the lid of the wooden commode-box just inside the door of the bunk room and relieved myself in the chamber-pot. As I closed the lid and turned back to bed, I heard Cuppy and the ship's carpenter, Hawley, snoring away. I automatically glanced in the direction of Koro's bunk—only to find it empty.

It had to be well past midnight. Where could he possibly be? Still more than a little drunk, I decided to go in search of my friend. As I made my way above deck, I could tell by the angle of the stars in the sky that it was early Christmas morn, perhaps an hour or two before the dawn. The boat was eerily silent and I saw no one moving about, as Captain Solomon had relieved the night watch of their duties.

As I made my way to the prow of the ship, I spotted a pair of canvas pants, neatly folded into a square, resting on the portside deck, atop which sat a tidily folded wool watch cap. There was no doubt in my mind as to whom the garments belonged to. I looked around, hoping to see some sign of Koro. Then I heard the sound of something splashing in the water below. I looked over the rail and was surprised to see Koro swimming in the open ocean, as easily as you or I might swim in a pond. Suddenly a fin broke the surface and sped in his direction. But before I could call out a warning, a small spume of spray shot forth from the top of the sleek gray shape's head, followed by a series of telltale clicks and squeals. As the porpoise drew closer to where Koro was swimming, it shot out of the water, pirouetting in mid-air, as if propelled by sheer joy, its wet hide glistening like a polished stone in the early morning starlight.

The harpooner did not seem in the least surprised by the dolphin's arrival, or concerned by its close proximity. Instead, he laughed, as one would upon greeting an old friend one has not seen in many years. To my surprise, as the animal swam past him, Koro reached out and grabbed its dorsal fin. Not only did the porpoise not seem to mind such familiarity, it willingly pulled Koro along behind it as if this was the most natural thing in the world. Even from such a distance and in such poor light, I could see the look of delight on Koro's face as his aquatic playmate sped through the water.

Then, without warning, the dolphin sounded, taking Koro along with him. I expected my friend to abandon his game and quickly resurface upon realizing the porpoise was headed for deeper water, but his head did not pop up above the waves. A minute passed, followed by another, and still there was no sign of Koro. Trying to control the panic I felt rising in my heart, I hurried over to the starboard rail, to see if perhaps the dolphin had carried the native underneath the ship and taken him to the other side, but there was no sign of him there, as well. I dashed back to where I had last seen my friend, trying to decide if I should raise the alarm of 'Man Overboard!', and whether it would do any good even if I did.

Just as I was about to give myself over to despair of ever seeing my friend again, a pair of cavorting dolphins leapt from the water, somersaulting in mid-air. I was so amazed I momentarily forgot all about Koro and, instead, watched, slack-jawed, as the aquatic tumblers splashed back down into the water. A moment or so later, Koro's bald head popped back up above the waves, gleaming like a pearl. Apparently unharmed and no worse for being underwater for over five minutes, the islander swam back to the ship and, grabbing hold of the anchor chain, began to climb back onto the *Absolom*.

I dropped back from the railing before Koro could catch sight of me. Whatever his reasons for indulging in his strange pre-dawn swim, they were none of my business. Besides, I sensed that what I had just witnessed was never meant to be seen by civilized eyes. What was it that he had he said earlier? *'My people also honor our god, Tangaroa, Lord of the Ocean, with celebration.'*

I hurried back to my bunk room in steerage and returned to my berth. If Cuppy or Hawley noticed my absence, they gave no sign of it. A few minutes later Koro entered and crawled into his bunk, still smelling of the sea.

Chapter Ten

The Sugar Bowl—Mulogo's Wager—To The Boats
Koro Stabs The Whale—Man Overboard!

It was a couple of weeks into the new year, and I had all but forgotten Koro's strange Christmas morning swim. We were seated at the table in the main galley, breaking our fast. I was wedged, as usual, between Koro and Mr. Hawley and seated opposite Mulogo. The African scowled at us by way of greeting, as he did most every morning. He had never been the friendliest of the harpooners, but since Koro came aboard his temperament had soured even further.

Pedro, the cook, set down a large pot of fresh coffee in the middle of the table. Then, to everyone's surprise, he placed a small bowl of sugar lumps down beside it. Normally sugar and butter were reserved for the officer class, but on rare occasions the Cap'n would indulge the skilled hands and harpooners as a reward.

Mulogo grinned and reached for the sugar bowl, only to have Pedro slap away his hand. "Cap'n say only Koro get sugar," the cook said in heavily accented English. "It his reward for killin' more whale."

"I kill as many whale as Koro does!" Mulogo retorted angrily.

"Cap'n not say Mulogo get sugar. He say *Koro* get sugar," the cook said sternly, waving a cleaver in the African's face.

Mulogo grudgingly drew back his hand, for fear of losing it to Pedro's knife skills.

"Go ahead," I said, nudging Koro with my elbow. "Claim your reward."

He warily eyed the sugar bowl as if it was a strange and potentially dangerous animal. "What do I do?" he asked.

"Put it in your coffee," I replied. "Just like you do with the molasses."

Koro tentatively picked up one of the lumps of sugar, turning it around between his thumb and forefinger, as if studying it, before dropping it in his coffee. Pedro promptly snatched the sugar bowl off the table and whisked it back to its hiding place in the ship's pantry, where it safely resided under lock and key. The entire table sat in silence, their own meals forgotten, and watched as Koro lifted the cup of sugared coffee to his lips and took a long sip.

"So—how is it?" I asked.

"Too sweet," he replied with a grimace as he set the tin cup back down.

After finishing out meal, we trooped out of the galley and onto the deck. Once we were in the open, Mulogo turned to face Koro. "I bet I kill the next whale before you do, Islander!" he said angrily.

"What are you willing to wager then?" I sneered in response. "It's not a proper bet unless you have something to lose."

Mulogo reached into his pocket and withdrew a watch, holding it up so that everyone could see. The case was much-worn and bore more than a few scratches, but it was obvious to the naked eye that it was gold. "Is this good enough?" he asked.

"It will do," I conceded. I glanced at Koro, who was observing the proceedings with a concerned look on his face. "What say you, my friend? Do you accept Mulogo's wager?"

"I do not have anything of value," he replied simply.

"You needn't worry, I am more than willing to stake you," I laughed. "I gladly bet my good luck charm that you will be first to kill the next whale!"

"You must not do that, Jonas!" Koro gasped, an alarmed look on his face. "That talisman is your protection!"

"It's all right," I assured him, patting the amulet as if it would soothe him as well. "The Cap'n's right: you *are* the finest harpooner on this ship. Every iron you throw finds its mark. I have perfect faith in you, Koro."

As if on cue, a voice sang out from high in the crow's nest overhead: *"Thar she blows! Whale off the starboard bow!"*

Upon hearing the cry, the *Absolom's* crew burst into action, each officer yelling for his crew to man and launch the boats. Suddenly the decks were swarming with men, like ants crawling over a picnic lunch.

It turned out that the *Absolom* had sailed up on a small pod of Right whales that fine January morning. Although the oil rendered from the blubber of such animals wasn't worth as much as Sperm oil, it was still of high quality. More importantly, the Rights strained the meals they took from the sea with mouths full of baleen—the stuff used to make buggy whips, umbrella ribs, and the stays in ladies' corsets.

Personally, I preferred hunting Rights, as they were quite docile, as such creatures go, and tended not to shy away from the boats. The Sperm Whales, on the other hand, were predators by nature, and, as such, knew a hunt when they saw it. Also, the Rights, once killed, float in the water and are much easier to tow back to the ship, whereas it was a struggle to keep a Sperm afloat from the moment it was slain.

The news of the wager between Mulogo and Koro had spread amongst the hands faster than cholera. There nothing like a contest of skill to stir the blood of sailors, especially those bored from being too long at sea, and the oarsmen of each whale boat were determined to do whatever it took to help claim the honor of the first kill for their respective harpooner. That is why, compared to the other officers, the whale boats piloted by Captain Solomon and Mr. Godward flew across the waves. I was rowing so fast my good luck charm was tapping against my breastbone like a door knocker. Every so often I would spare a sidewise glance towards Mr. Godward's boat, only to see my opposite number glowering back at me.

Of course, Captain Solomon and Mr. Godward knew nothing about the wager between their harpooners, or what was at stake, for such things are above the officers. But if either man was surprised by their crew's eagerness for the hunt, neither of them showed any interest in finding out why.

Our prey was a large cow, placidly feeding on krill, much like its four-footed counterpart would graze in a meadow. Like all Rights, she had a rotund body, an arching rostrum, dark-gray skin and rough, white patches atop her head, and an exceptionally broad back. As we got within striking distance, the Captain sang out and Koro took his stand. As he did so, Mr. Godward's boat suddenly shot forward, bringing them a good fifty feet closer to the target. To my surprise, I saw that Mulogo was already in position, framed against the hard blue sky of the Pacific like a proud African prince, his harpoon drawn back in preparation of its murderous flight.

Mulogo hurled his harpoon with all his considerable might, striking the whale in the shoulder blade. The men in Mr. Godward's boat let out a loud huzzah to celebrate their man landing the first strike. In response, the hands in our boat once more grabbed oars and shot forward another hundred feet.

"Have you fools gone mad?" Captain Solomon shouted. *"We're too close to the damned thing!"* As my back was to the whale, I did not see what happened next. However, I did have an unobstructed view of the look of horror and amazement that crossed Captain Solomon's face as he cried out: *"Merciful God! Koro! What are you doing?"*

No longer able to contain myself, I shipped my oars and turned about to see what could so shock a man who had seen everything the ocean could possibly cough up, only to find my friend no longer in the bow of the whaleboat. My first thought was that he had fallen afoul of the line, like poor Haraldson before him, and had been jerked into the sea—then I realized that Koro had yet to throw his harpoon.

"I've never seen anything like it!" Captain Solomon exclaimed. "He jumped twenty feet from a standing start, right onto the damned beast's back! The damn fool heathen is going to get his-self killed, and us in the bargain!"

It was then I saw Koro on the swimming whale, armed with one of the killing irons used to sever the arteries. He was racing along its back in a dead run in the direction of the beast's head. Without thinking, I got to my feet and shouted at the top of my lungs: *"Koro! No!"*

If my friend heard my words above the rush and roar of the whale, he did not heed them. He raised the lance on high and plunged it with both hands into the Right's neck. A gout of blood instantly burst forth from the creature's blowhole, followed by it surging forward in a panicked attempt to flee whatever was attacking it. The water was instantly churned into chop rough enough to raise the bow of the whaleboat several feet in the air and then slam it back down again, like an angry child playing with a toy.

One moment I was standing in the boat, the next I was flying through the air while the bloody spume from the wounded whale fell upon me like scarlet rain. I heard Nicodemus sing out *"Man overboard!"* but this time it seemed so far, far away. It wasn't until the salt water closed over my head, pouring itself into my nose, ears and throat, that I realized he meant *me*.

Part Four

Terror Comes Aboard

Chapter Eleven

Saved From A Watery Grave—News From The Pilgrimage—Marcus Feeds The Sharks

Even as I was hurled from the captain's boat into the open ocean, I knew rescue would not be soon in coming. The fish had yet to go flukes up, and until it did so, none of the whaleboats could be bothered to collect me. It may seem a cruel decision to place the death of a fish above the life of a man, but for the *Absolom* to lose a whale would affect every member of the crew, while the loss of a single hand would, for the most part, not reverberate beyond his bride and kin. Assuming he had either to mourn his passing in the first place.

Luckily, I knew how to swim, but there is a difference between the mill pond of my youth and the Pacific. I struggled mightily to keep my head above water, which had been made angry and bloody by the death throes of the hunted whale. But it was as if my clothes, and, in particular, my boots, had been transformed into lead, and I was pulled inexorably downward. It seemed as if the ocean floor had claimed me for its own, and was drawing me to its dark, wet bosom. The next thing I knew, the waves had closed over my head, reducing the sun's fierce, burning glare to a distant, flickering disc of light.

As I sank downward, I could hear the splash of my shipmates' oars and the shout of their voices, muted and warped by the water that surrounded me on all sides. I also heard the eerie moan of the dying whale, carried through the sea just as the cries of a four-legged beast would travel through the air. My lungs began to burn, and as I wrapped my hands about the dolphin amulet still looped about my neck, I heard Uncle Cal's voice in my ear, telling me how it would keep me safe from the dangers of the sea.

Suddenly I saw a shadow cutting through the water in my direction. And although I was well on my way to death's door, my heart still managed to leap with terror. As far as every sailor is considered, it is better to drown than to be torn to bloody bits by sharks. If ever a man was caught between the devil and the deep blue sea, it was I at that very moment.

But just as my lungs could no longer contain themselves, I realized that the sleek figure swimming towards me was not that of a shark, but a dolphin. There was something trailing from its mouth, and at first I thought it was a small squid or some other type of fish it was dining on. Then I realized, just as the ocean rushed in to fill my lungs, that what it held clutched in its jaws was a woolen watch cap.

The next thing I knew, I was staring at the bottom of a whaleboat as strong, callused hands pressed against my ribs from behind. I abruptly coughed and vomited up a foul mixture of salt water and bile. I pulled myself onto the rowing bench and nodded a heartfelt thank-you to Nicodemus, who had been the one to resuscitate me.

"How you feelin', Padgett?" Captain Solomon asked from his seat at the tiller.

"Lucky to be alive, sir," I replied truthfully.

"I dare say you are," he agreed. "I'd given you up for drown't, to tell truth. Koro as well, the mad islander! When you went flyin' into the drink, Koro jumped off the whale after you! But I'll be damned if ten minutes later he don't come swimmin' up, bare as Adam, save for his tattoos and that damned cap of his, and pushes you over the gunwales!"

"Koro—isn't dead—?" I asked in astonishment. Seeing how the last I saw of my friend, he had leapt onto the back of a swimming whale and plunged his harpoon deep enough to pierce the beast's heart, I could be forgiven my surprise.

"He certainly seems lively enough to me," Captain Solomon said, gesturing to the bow of the boat with the stem of his pipe.

I turned and saw Koro seated in the bow behind me, dripping water and naked save for the sodden watch cap covering his hairless head. My friend grinned at me, as if everything that had just happened had been nothing more than a schoolboy's lark.

"Mulogo just lost his pocket watch," he announced proudly. "But tell me, Jonas—what do you do with such a thing?"

I will give Mulogo credit—he surrendered his pocket watch to Koro with far greater grace than I would have thought possible. Koro, for his part, did not gloat or seek to humiliate his fellow harpooner. However, being a savage, while he might not have understood the actual function of the pocket watch, he most assuredly grasped its significance. He fashioned a cord from a strip of leather and used it to hang the trophy about his neck.

And every day, when we took our meals in the mess, Mulogo was forced to look across the galley table and know who the greatest harpooner ever to walk the decks of the *Absolom* truly was.

I know people who read travelogues tend to envision the oceans as vast, empty expanses, but, in truth, the whaling and shipping routes are well traveled by vessels of every make and flag, and it was a rare week when we did not spy another ship, whether merchant or military, off our bow.

Some of these we gave a wide berth, especially those flying flags of the more quarrelsome countries. And it would seem others made a point of avoiding us a well, if for no other reason than the smell and grease from our try-works. But for the most part, there was usually a ritual greeting between the captains, a formal tipping of the hat, if you will, and a brief exchange of news from the mainland or warnings of foul weather or treacherous reefs, most of it conducted via hailing horns.

It was after dinner, and I was taking my ease on the weather deck, enjoying the sunset before retiring to my bunk, when I heard one of the hands sing out: *"Ship off the starboard bow!"*

Captain Solomon came out of his quarters with his spy glass in his hand, and raised it to his remaining eye. "'Tis the

Pilgrimage, out of Nantucket!" he exclaimed. "She's captained by Abner Fastnacht—we shipped together on the *Bonnie Belle*, long years ago."

In ten minutes' time the *Pilgrimage* was parallel with the *Absolom*, with no more than a hundred yards between us. The captain ducked back into his quarters and returned with his hailing horn, which amplified his voice. *"Ahoy, Pilgrimage!"*

"Ahoy, Absolom!" came the response. Captain Fastnacht—a stout fellow with once-golden hair and whiskers now turned silver—stood on the poop deck of his ship, armed with his own hailing horn. "Haven't seen ye in dog's years! How's the mizzus?"

"Alive, last time I was home! And yourself?"

"She died of the influenza!"

"Sorry to hear that, Abner!"

"I got me a new one now," Fastnacht replied with a shrug. "She's younger and prettier, but nowhere the cook the last one was!"

"Where are you headed?"

"Back to Chile! We're in sore need of fresh hands! We have barely enough crew to make it back to Valparaiso as it is!"

"Are you poxed, man?"Captain Solomon asked in alarm, his eyes searching the *Pilgrimage's* rigging for sign of the tell-tale yellow and black plague flag.

"You see no yellow jacket flying from my mast, do ye?" Fastnacht replied indignantly.

"I meant no offense!" Captain Solomon assured his old friend. "What of the whales in these waters? Have you seen sign of King Jim?"

"That I have, God have mercy on my soul!" The *Pilgrimage's* captain exclaimed. "I lost twenty good men to that black devil less than a week ago! He stove in four of my whale boats and drowned all the mates, save the bo'sun! He's the reason we're headed back to the mainland!"

"Where was this?" Captain Solomon asked, unable to hide the excitement in his voice.

"Three hundred miles southwest of Rapa Nui! He's

traveling with a harem—larger than any I've ever seen! But it's not worth it, Wendell! Mark my words! The fish is big as an island and black as Death itself! There's no lance forged that can pierce that monster's heart!"

"I thank you for the warning, Abner! Godspeed!"

"Farewell to ye, as well, Wendell!" Captain Fastnacht responded. As the *Pilgrimage* passed from sight, I saw its captain sadly shake his head, the way one does when you know wise words have fallen on deaf ears.

As for Captain Solomon, he lost no time in hurrying back to his quarters to chart a new course. One, no doubt, that would take us southwest of Rapa Nui, known to the white world as Easter Island.

Two days later, we came upon a small pod of right whales. But this time, after my previous escape from Davy Jones' locker, Captain Solomon decided it might not be wise to risk his cooper on the hunt, and replaced me in the whaleboat. Although I admit to missing the excitement of the chase, I was glad to surrender my place at the oars, as hauling back a dead whale is the most onerous task known to Man.

Of course, it was not as if I was lolling about on soft pillows and eating bon-bons while my shipmates were out among the whales. There is much that must be done to convert a ship into a floating slaughterhouse and oil refinery, and I spent most of my time knocking together the barrels and casks I knew would be soon needed, as well as helping Cuppy set up the try works.

As to be expected, thanks to Koro, the Captain's boat claimed the first kill and was also the first to return with its prize. Once everyone had sufficiently recovered from their row back to the ship, the business of cutting in began in earnest. As usual, Marcus worked the carcass, using the flensing spade to slice the blubber off the whale in blanket pieces, and then attaching it to the hook so it could be hauled on board and taken below decks to the blubber room. The West Indian sang as he did his bloody work in a strong, lilting voice:

"The one shirt I have, ratta cut ahm,
Same place him patch, ratta cut ahm,
Rain, rain oh! Rain, rain oh!
Rain, rain oh, fall down an' wet me up!"

Then, upon finishing his song, Marcus turned—or so I was told, as I was not there to see it—and urinated onto the sharks gathered to feed on the butchered whale, as was his custom. But this time something went wrong—perhaps he lost his footing, or something in the water jostled the floating carcass on which he stood. Whatever the reason, Marcus plummeted from his perch and landed among the feeding sharks. Although I did not see him fall, I *did* hear him cry out—it was the scream of a man who knows he is going to his death in the worst way imaginable.

"*Man overboard!*" Jones the Orkneyman shouted, although we all knew there was no hope of rescue even as he spoke the words.

Koro and I ran to the starboard rail, arriving just in time to see poor Marcus burst up out of the sea, as if standing upright. A shark had come up from underneath him, and had his legs in its mouth. Marcus' death shriek was as primal and awful as the beast that had seized him. As the doomed man beat his fists against the thing's snout in a futile attempt to escape, a second shark leapt from the water and seized his upper half, tearing him open like a Christmas cracker.

As the second shark swam away with Marcus' lifeless upper body clamped in its dreadful jaws, I noticed that it bore a wicked scar along one side of its head, and that it was missing its right eye.

Chapter Twelve

In Search of King Jim—A Rude Awakening—Wither Levant?—The Shadow Of Suspicion— The Middle Watch

As Marcus left no mortal remains to say prayers over, Captain Solomon was forced to make do by having the mates gather the crew in the waist of the ship and reading a passage from the Good Book. Once he was done, he snapped the Bible shut and gave us all a stern look.

"As you all may know, since you gossip among yourselves worse than a gaggle of old biddies at a quiltin' bee, I have been in search of King Jim—the most treacherous whale that swims these Southern Seas. And now I have a clue as to where to find him!"

As the gathered sailors muttered uncertainly amongst themselves at this proclamation, I looked to Mr. Godward, who stood at the captain's side on the poopdeck. The first mate's face was unreadable; although his jaw was clenched so tight I could see the muscle jump.

"I know there are some of you who call King Jim a devil!" Captain Solomon continued. "And others, still, who think him a god. But in my eyes he's just another fish! Meaner and bigger than most, but a fish all the same! And I have yet to meet a thing that swims in the ocean that I *can't* kill! But the truth is what I'm *really* after ain't King Jim, but his harem! Like any proper monarch, he travels with an entourage— one said to number in the hundreds! If we find King Jim's harem, boys, we can fill our holds to overflowing in record time! Who among you would rather spend next Christmas Day on dry land, with your loved ones, eatin' figgy puddin' and drinkin' wassail instead of dinin' on mince pies and grog?"

"*Aye!*" shouted fifty voices as one.

"Very good," Captain Solomon said with a smile. "And this evening, in memory of Marcus, I'm allowing each man a tot of rum!"

That last bit of news was good for another hurrah from the crew, who returned to their duties considerably cheered by the prospect of toasting their devoured shipmate come the evening meal.

A ship at sea, no matter what kind it might be, is rarely truly 'asleep'. The same was true for the *Absolom*. As soon as the ship was first under sail, we had been called aft for watch selection. Mr. Levant headed the starboard watch, and Mr. Shreve the port, and each mate chose from the crew who they wished to serve under them, and then divided them down even further into separate teams. Before my elevation to ship's cooper, I had served port watch—assigned four hours for sleep and four for work, throughout the twenty- four. Once a watch is done, it is sent below, if not to sleep, then to keep out of the way of their replacements. Save for special occasions, the only time the entire crew was awake and above decks at the same time was the dog watch, when we took our meals.

That night, after toasting Marcus, I retired to my bunk, knowing I would have to be back up and about come midnight, making yet more barrels for still more oil, until the blubber rooms below deck were empty. I had just fallen into a deep sleep when I found myself roughly shaken awake by the bos'un, Gusset.

"All hands on deck! The Captain wants a head count!"

"What in damnation for?" Hawley, the ship's carpenter, snarled. He, too, was resentful of being dragged from his bunk before his appointed watch.

"We're missin' a couple of men," Gusset replied tersely.

Hawley and I exchanged puzzled looks. Given the harsh working conditions and piss-poor pay for a whaler, it's wasn't unusual for three or four men to jump ship every voyage; but normally they waited until the ship put into port or dropped anchor at an inhabited island. Where was there to run to in the middle of the ocean? We were thousands of miles from land in any given direction.

Grumbling, Hawley and I threw on our clothes and made our way to the weather deck, where we found the rest of the crew gathered in the waist of the ship. Mr. Shreve and Mr. Gusset walked among the ranks, lanterns in hand, staring hard at our faces, clothes and hands, while Mr. Godward took the harpooners below decks to inspect the holds. As I looked around, I realized that I had yet to see Mr. Levant, he of the bristling brows.

Meanwhile, Captain Solomon stood atop the poopdeck and called the roll like a headmaster. Each man, in turn, answered to his name save two: the Algonquin known as Askuwheteau and a Yorkshireman named Swinton. When Mr. Godward and his team returned from their search below decks, he went to speak to the captain, and the two retired to his cabin.

"You men off-watch, go back to your berths," Mr. Shreve commanded, before quickly heading off to join his fellow officers aft.

Both weary and perplexed, I did as ordered and headed back to my bunkroom with Hawley. Upon returning, I found Cuppy and Koro there as well. The old blacksmith was covered in reeking soot from overseeing the try-works' fires, which were fueled by the skins of slaughtered whales.

"What do you make of the cap'n's headcount?" I asked.

"I hear that Levant's missing as well," Cuppy said darkly. "Whatever happened to 'em, they didn't desert."

"Perhaps they went overboard?" I suggested.

"In a calm sea?" Hawley replied doubtfully.

"I overheard Gusset tell Mr. Shreve there was blood splashed all over the bow, near the anchor chain," the old blacksmith said.

"Maybe Askuwheteau got too much rum in him tonight and killed Swinton and Mr. Levant," Hawley asked. "You know how Red Indians are when it comes to liquor."

"It's possible," Cuppy replied with a shrug. "I remember, twenty years back, there was a hand on the old *S.S. Gallant* who went stark, staring mad. Got up in the middle of the night and slit the throats of every man asleep in the fo'c'sle."

"If Askuwheteau did such a thing, he's got to still be on board." I turned to look at Koro. "Did you find anything below decks?"

"Nothing but rats," Koro replied, with a shake of his head.

"Maybe he slew Swinton and Levant in a fit of drunken rage and hurled them into the ocean, then jumped in after?" Hawley suggested.

"But why would he do such a thing, drunk or not?" I asked.

"Who knows what possesses a heathen to do anything?" the carpenter replied with a shrug. "No offense, Koro."

"Well, all I know is that I have another hour before I go back weather side," I grunted as I crawled into my bunk. "And wherever Mr. Levant and the others may be, it most certainly is not here."

Three hours later, I was once more up and about my business, and half-way into what is called the Middle Watch, which runs from midnight to four in the morning. My cooper's bench was set up in the waist of the ship, between the fore and main masts, and all around me the work of the ship went on as always, mysterious disappearances or not.

It takes three days, laboring around the clock, to cut in and try out a whale. During this time, the decks become incredibly greasy, until they're as slick as a frozen pond. If not for the amount of blood found before the mast, I would have had no problem believing the missing hands had slipped and fallen overboard while no one was looking.

The try-works, which belched out billows of grease-laden smoke into the night sky, also provided the light by which we labored. Bundles of scrap— hard, brittle lumps of blubber that's had the oil boiled out of them—burned in an iron basket swung between the twin chimneys, producing a flaring yellow blaze that gave us plenty of light to work by, while also throwing eerie, distorted shadows.

Mr. Shreve stood on the poop deck, overseeing the watch, since, unlike the rest of us aboard the *Absolom*, Captain Solomon was allowed the privilege of sleeping eight hours at a stretch. The only real difference the strange disappearance of Mr. Levant and the two hands had made was the addition of the Colt Paterson revolver the Second Mate now wore on his hip.

After awhile, Shreve climbed down the ladder from the poopdeck and headed forward, past the try-works, to check on the bow. As I was busy with the work at hand, I did not give it much thought, until, a few moments later, there came a shout of alarm, followed by first a gun-shot then a scream of terror, the likes of which put poor, departed Marcus to shame.

As I turned toward the bow of the ship, I freed my knife from my belt and picked up the adze I used to smooth the wood, hefting it as a savage would a war-club. Just then Shreve staggered out of the leaping shadows beyond the foremast, his eyes wide with horror and his face white as the death that was on its way to claim him. There was no sign of the gun he had been carrying earlier—nor his right arm.

Chapter Thirteen

The Boarding Party—Blood on the Decks
One-Eye Claims His Due

As the hapless Second Mate collapsed onto the deck, his life's blood pumping from the raw stump of his shoulder, there emerged from the darkness at the bow of the ship things vomited from a madman's nightmare.

They walked on two legs, just like men, but there all resemblance to humanity halted. Their skin was grayish-blue, still shining and wet from the sea, and their heads jutted forward, parallel with their hunched shoulders. Their faces were a hideous admixture of shark and man, with pointed noses, gaping, lipless mouths filled with jagged teeth, and eyes as black and round as shoe-buttons. Along their necks were pulsating gills, and in their heavily webbed hands they clutched koa spears studded with shark teeth.

At the very head of the monstrous boarding party stood their leader. Although much changed from last I saw him, I recognized the scarred face and withered eye, and knew that this was the leader of the savages who had killed my friends on Nuka Hiva, the cannibal chieftain I had come to call One-Eye.

"Mother of Christ!" Jones the Orkneyman shouted in horror. "They're climbing up the anchor chain!"

"*All hands on deck!*" Mr. Godward bellowed. "*All hands on deck!*"

As if in answer, One-Eye gave voice to a roaring war-cry and shook his toothed spear as the rest of the boarding party charged across the foredeck and into the waist of the ship. At that exact moment, the hatch to the fo'c'sle was thrown open by the hands responding to Mr. Godward's call, only to be immediately set upon by the invaders. While their brothers pursued the retreating sailors into the forecastle like terriers chasing rats, the other shark-men swarmed the try-works, only to be met by old Cuppy and his men, who used the six-foot long bailers to hurl ladles of boiling whale oil at their attackers. One of the monsters shrieked in agony upon catching a face full of scalding liquid, yet still threw his spear, piercing the torso of the nearest sailor.

One of the hideous beasts lunged at me, but I managed to side-step his attack and brought the adze down, burying the blade deep in the cartilage of his snout, while I also drove my knife into one of his eyes. Having dispatched the fiend, I quickly retreated to the quarterdeck, where my shipmates were making their stand.

"*God in Three Persons!*" Captain Solomon bellowed as he emerged from his cabin, dressed in nothing but long johns, boots and the gun belt buckled about his waist. "What's this madness?"

"We're under attack by demons, sir!" the First Mate replied, his face the color of cold oatmeal.

"Demons?" the captain scoffed as he aimed his revolver and fired down at one of the invaders, blowing a hole in the shark-man's torso. "They're just natives in Tiki masks, nothing more! For God's sake man, I thought you had more sense than that!" He then turned and yelled at Mr. Gusset, who was watching the slaughter play out before him with bulging eyes. "Don't just stand there gawking, bo'sun! Go below and break-out the long guns from the armory cabinet! Take Godward with you!"

"Aye-aye, Cap'n!" both men replied, and quickly disappeared.

The dreadful boarding party pressed forward, undeterred by Solomon's gunfire, and was met by crew members armed with whatever tool they had at hand. I saw Jones take a spear to the gut from one of the shark-men and drop to his knees as if saying his prayers. The creature that struck the blow opened wide his mouth and snapped the Orkneyman's head clean off at the shoulders as easily as you would bite off the end of a cigar.

The Classics, Homer and Virgil, stood side by side, stabbing at the creatures with the harpoons they made their living by. But one of the monsters, spotting the manacle on Homer's ankle, grabbed the dangling length of chain and yanked the escaped slave's feet out from under him. Homer screamed in terror as the shark-man raced back toward the bow of the ship, dragging the harpooner along the oil-slicked deck behind him like a child pulling a toy sled.

"Stand your ground, men!" Captain Solomon shouted as he slid down the ladder feet-first to join his crew on the quarterdeck. *"Drive the devils back into the sea!"*

Another of the were-sharks lunged at me, gnashing his teeth as he thrust his spear at my nethers. I leapt back, only to slip on the oily deck and land my back, knocking the wind from my sails. The creature grinned as best it could with such wicked daggers wedged in its mouth, and lifted its spear, eager to drive it into my exposed belly.

Suddenly there was a wild shout and Koro leapt forth, seemingly from nowhere, slashing at the two-legged shark with one of the flensing spades, opening my attacker up from shoulder to crotch and spilling his innards onto the deck. Without a moment's pause, the islander reached down and yanked me back onto my feet. Koro and I then stood back-to-back, blocking and parrying spear thrusts with the tools of our trade, while all around us our friends and shipmates did the same. Everywhere there was blood and screams, both human and inhuman.

I saw Captain Solomon, in the thick of the battle, cursing a blue streak as he fired at the abominations assaulting his crew. From the look on his face, I knew the old sea captain realized that he was fighting something far worse than cannibals wearing masks. Suddenly, One-Eye rose up before him, showing every tooth in a wicked snarl. Captain Solomon pointed his Colt at the were-shark's head. One-Eye froze, and something like apprehension flickered across his inhuman face. Captain Solomon pulled the trigger...

And the hammer came down on an empty chamber with a dreadful clicking sound.

With an exultant growl, One-Eye knocked Captain Solomon's gun out of his hand, plunging his spear into his opponent's right eye socket with such force the point burst through the back of Solomon's skull as if in were a melon. I cried out as I saw my captain fall lifeless to the blood-wet deck, as if the killing blow had struck me as well.

One-Eye grasped the haft of his spear with his webbed hand and yanked it free, holding it aloft as he roared in triumph. His fellow Mako Kanaka froze in mid-battle at the sound, swinging their heads in the direction of their leader. Moving as one, the shark-men began to retreat, backing slowly towards the bow.

Suddenly, there was the crack of rifle fire and the smell of gun powder and the head of one of the shark-men disappeared in an explosion of brains and cartilage. I turned and saw Mr. Godward, Gusset, Mulogo and others, armed with long guns, emerging from one of the hatches towards the stern of the vessel.

"Shoot!" Mr. Godward shouted. "Kill them all!"

As the *Absolom's* defenders opened fire, the orderly withdrawal of the Mako Kanaka became a rout. The shark-men dropped their weapons and fled for the bulwarks, only to fall in a hail of bullets. Those closest to the railing died in mid-transformation, flopping on the deck like landed fish, their legs fused together below the hip.

The only Mako Kanaka to escape the initial volley unharmed was One-Eye, who used the chaos to flee to the bow. Koro and I gave chase, unmindful of the bullets still flying through the air. A murderous rage filled my heart, unlike anything I have ever known before or since. This monster was responsible for the deaths of men I considered companions and friends; and, in the case of Captain Solomon, he had murdered the only person I held in as high esteem as my own, beloved uncle. At that moment I wanted One-Eye's death more than a starving man wants food, or a drowning man wants air, and I would not be sated until I saw the fiend's blood. But, just as we closed in on him, he clambered out onto the bowsprit extending from the prow of the ship and hurled himself into ocean below.

Koro and I ran to the rail and stared down into the water.

One-Eye had cast aside his humanoid guise as easily as you or I would toss aside a garment, and was now gliding only a few feet below the surface like a gray ghost. The were-shark turned slightly on his left side to look up at his enemies peering down upon him, daring us to follow him into his element.

"The bastard is taunting us!" I spat. "He's not even trying to run away!"

Koro snatched up a harpoon, jumped onto the bulwarks, and let fly the iron, sinking it up to the wooden haft in One-Eye's back with such force the spear-point stuck out the other side. The Mako Kanaka thrashed mightily, lashing the sea into white froth, but the harpoon could not be loosed, and after a few minutes the were-shark ceased his struggles and floated belly up.

It wasn't long before other sharks came swimming up to feed on One-Eye's carcass. Whether they were true sharks, or his own people, it is impossible to say.

Part Five

Ocean Born

Chapter Fourteen

A Terrible Silence—Sailcloth Shrouds—A Funeral At Sea—
Captain Godward Names His Mates
Mulogo Swings The Cat

Having survived the attempted boarding, the remaining crew of the *Absolom* set about collecting the dead and washing the decks of blood. It was a sad and gruesome task, and one undertaken in near silence. The horrors I and my shipmates had undergone that dreadful night had stunned us so thoroughly not one of us could speak more than the most basic of instructions.

As we hurled the monstrous carcasses of our attackers back into the sea from which they'd climbed, I saw something dangerously close to madness in the eyes of many of the crew. I could tell by the tightness at the corners of the men's mouths and the trembling of their hands that their silence was out of fear that speaking aloud might lead to screaming—a screaming they might be powerless to stop.

When the final tally was made it revealed the *Absolom* had lost seven good men that horrid night: Captain Solomon, Mr. Shreve, Jones the Orkneyman, Homer, and three able-bodies from the fo'c'sle. Taking into account the missing Third Mate, the redskin Askuwheteau and Swinton the Yorkshireman who, no doubt, fell victim to the devils' scouting party, the true reckoning was ten.

A bolt of sailcloth was brought up from below decks and cut into seven lengths, and Mr. Gussett and a couple of deckhands began stitching together long canvas bags, into which the bodies of the fallen were placed, one by one, along with with a weight of brick. Each dead man had suffered the most gruesome mutilations imaginable: poor Shreve had lost an arm; Homer was missing the leg that had borne his old slave shackle; Captain Solomon was now blinded in both eyes, and the only way we could identify the Orkneyman was by the tattoo on his chest. Looking upon them lying there, lined up like so many broken toys, filled my heart with a profound grief.

Although I had been on good standing with them all, I felt the loss of Mr. Shreve and Captain Solomon most keenly. The Second Mate had always treated me square, and I found him to be a likable, solid-sort of man. And as for my captain, I had grown almost as fond of him as my dear, departed Uncle Calvin. My only solace was the knowledge that he had died as any good captain should—fighting alongside his men, defending his ship to the last of his breath.

Come the dawn, all hands were called on deck and together carried the bodies down on the main deck, placing them with their feet to the sea. The gang plank was removed from the rail and the Captain's shrouded body placed upon it. We stood gathered in the waist of the ship, with solemn faces and uncovered heads as the rising sun turned the sky a burnished gold.

Mr. Godward, the *Absolom's* only surviving officer, came forward, his back stiff and straight as a ram-rod. "We are gathered here, under the eye of God, to say farewell to these, our shipmates and masters," he said in a loud voice. "They died bravely, every one of them, defending the ship against crazed, cannibal natives..."

I and a couple of my fellow shipmates raised our heads at that point in the eulogy and exchanged glances with one other, uncertain if we had heard our new captain correctly, but did not speak up.

"But none fought as valiantly as her captain," Godward continued, and there was a chorus of assent from the crew. "He ruled the *Absolom* as wisely and justly as his namesake. Never have I shipped with a man who knew more about the ways of the ocean, and the things that swim in it, than Wendell Solomon. He died as he lived—like a whaler."

Godward opened the Bible he held clutched in his hands: "As it says in Psalms, Chapter Eight, Verses Six through Nine: 'Thou madest him to have dominion over the work of Thy hands; Thou hast put all things under his feet; All sheep and oxen, yea, and the beasts of the field; The fowl of the air, and the fish of the sea, and whatsoever passeth through the paths of the seas. O Lord our Lord, how excellent is thy name in all the earth!'" This was followed by a heartfelt, if slightly baffled chorus of 'Amens', then the crew sang a couple verses of "Amazing Grace" before tilting the gang-plank upwards, sliding the shrouded corpse of Captain Wendell Solomon into the waiting ocean, where it plunged beneath the waves and sank without a trace. This ritual was repeated another six times, although words were only spoken over the bodies of Mr. Shreve, Homer, and the Orkneyman, the remainder being consigned to Davey Jones Locker in anonymity.

As the last of the *Absolom's* slain disappeared below the foam, Mr. Godward turned to address the assembled crew: "As all of you are gathered here, I will go ahead and announce my mates. As you well know, the attack by the cannibals robbed us of nearly all our officers. Until such time as we can make for Peru, I shall have Mr. Gussett as my First Mate and Mulogo as my Second."

This last bit of news was greeted with scowls and dark mutters from the crew. Hawley the carpenter stepped forward. "I got no problem working alongside heathens and darkies, sir. But I'll be damned if I take orders from one, much less both," he said firmly.

"And I'll be damned if I am addressed in such a manner by a skilled hand," Godward replied curtly.

With just a nod from their new captain, a couple of hands pounced on Hawley, dragging the surprised carpenter to the nearest mast, where the shirt was torn from his back. He was then placed spread-eagled against the shrouds, his wrists tied to the rigging. Mulogo strutted forward, grinning in amusement as he watched Hawley struggle like a fly caught in a web. In one ebony hand, the *Absolom*'s newly minted Second Mate held a closed cat made of sound, thick rope, the end of which was tightly knotted. Mulogo took his place on the break of the deck, a few feet away from Hawley so that he could get in a good swing. He raised his muscular arm—the same one that he used to throw harpoons—and brought it down onto the hapless carpenter's naked back, bending his body as he did so in order to give the blow its full force.

Hawley jerked violently with each stroke of the lash, like a puppet on a string. On the third blow, blood began to seep from the welts across his back. By the fifth stripe, he cried out in a ragged voice: *"Jesus Christ! Deliver me, savior!"* But such entreaties meant nothing to Mulogo who, as Hawley himself had pointed out, was of a savage creed.

It wasn't until the poor devil swooned and went limp, his body held upright only by the bindings about his wrists that Godward finally ordered his Second to stay his hand. "That's enough!" he barked. "Take him down and put him in his bunk." The *Absolom*'s new captain then turned to face the rest of the men. "If there are any more of you who question my choice of Mates, you take it up with Mr. Mulogo. Is that clear?"

"Aye, Cap'n," the assembled hands said in sullen unison as they watched Mulogo shake the blood from the cat.

Chapter Fifteen

The Hunt Continues—The Ocean Born—The Drowned City

Given the depletion of our numbers, and the loss of so many of the ship's officers, it was assumed that the *Absolom* would follow the *Pilgrimage's* example and promptly set sail for Peru in order to replenish its crew. However, come the dogwatch, as we were gathered for the evening mess, it was announced that the ship would continue on the course charted by the late Captain Solomon.

"By my calculations, we are a day or so short of our final destination," Captain Godward informed the crew. "We're too close to give up now and turn back. It was Captain Solomon's wish that we find King Jim's harem, and that's how I plan to honor his memory. Are you with me, boys? Will you fill the holds with oil from the monster whale's wives so that the Widow Solomon shall know her good husband's death was not in vain?"

As he spoke, I could see each man was moved, as was I, by the thought of the captain's lady, tirelessly pacing the widow's walk, her eyes searching the horizon for sign of the *Absolom's* sails. Whalers may be rough, uncultured men, but there is also a strong streak of sentiment to be found in even the most salty dog, for rare is the sailor who does not have a mother, sweetheart or wife waiting news of their return.

"Aye!" cried the crew in unison save for one. "We are with you, sir!"

Who, you ask, was the sole hand who did not add his voice to the chorus? It was none other than Koro.

Later, as we prepared to bunk down, Koro asked me a question that had crossed my mind earlier: "Why did Mr. Godward claim the Mano Kanaka were cannibals?"

"Perhaps it was too much for him to accept," I replied, with a shrug of my shoulders. "Lord knows, I doubted my own sanity when I saw those things. It is far easier for him to explain an attack by cannibal natives than by men who turn into sharks—or sharks that turn into men. It is a hard thing for a civilized mind to wrap around without it altogether snapping. And he's *Captain* Godward now," I reminded my friend. "And you best not forget it if you don't want to end up like poor Hawley, there." I nodded to where the carpenter lay face down in his bunk, drifting in and out of delirium, courtesy of a fever and a laudanum-laced cup of grog. "But speaking of the Mano Kanaka—are we in danger of them returning?"

"No," Koro replied solemnly. "They will not return. Blood vengeance has been taken for the insult to their chief. Even if they desired to do further harm, they dare not follow us, for the *Absolom* has entered the waters of the Ocean Born. It is taboo to trespass. The Ocean Born are jealous of their territory—especially during mating season."

"What are the Ocean Born?"

"They are the ancestors of my people and the gods of the islands. Long ago, there were beings without form that mated with the creatures of the sea. Their children were the whale-lord Tangaroa, the octopus-god Kanaloa, the shark-god Dakuwaga, the eel-king Tunaroa, the sea-dragon Waka, the ray-god Punga, and Ikatere, lord of the dolphins. My people, the Naia, were born of Ikatere and young girls sacrificed to him by the islanders."

"So you're telling me you're descended from a dolphin?" I said with a laugh, unable to disguise my amusement.

"No," he corrected gently. "A dolphin *god*."

That night I dreamt of the Ocean Born.

In my dream, I was standing on the bow of the *Absolom*, naked save for the dolphin amulet about my neck. Above me the Milky Way filled the sky, its cold, distant fire reflected in the dark mirror of the water below. I suddenly became aware that I was not alone and turned to see Koro standing on the deck beside me. Save for his eternal watch cap, he, too, was naked, and the tattoos covering his hairless torso seemed to writhe with a life all their own.

Koro smiled and gestured for me to follow him as he climbed up onto the railing and jumped overboard. Without pause or fear I followed suit, plunging feet-first into the waiting ocean, just as I used to leap into the old mill pond back home. I sank like a stone, and the salt water flooded my lungs within seconds. But instead of drowning, I found myself breathing just as I would on land.

Koro could also breathe beneath the waves, of course. He smiled and took me by the hand, leading me deeper still, through water darker than any midnight I have ever known.

Down, down, down we went, into the vast, hidden belly of the deep, through sunken valleys and forests of seaweed that towered higher than any tree that grows on land. Although the sun's rays could never penetrate the darkness that surrounded us, I had no trouble seeing the wonders hidden so many leagues beneath the waves. Again, I attributed this to the nature of dreams.

At first I mistook the city for a submerged mountain range, but as we drew closer I realized that they were, instead, a collection of ziggurat-like structures covered in living coral. I was both exhilarated and terrified by the towering structures, which made the skyscrapers of New York City look like termite mounds in comparison, and I wondered what might dwell in such a fantastic and alien landscape?

As we swam between the gigantic step-pyramids, I glimpsed windows and doorways carved into the walls, and what appeared to be vast, boneless figures stirring sluggishly within the shadows. My heart leapt with fear, for I knew as only dreamers can, that what dwelt inside these mammoth edifices were the shapeless beings who spawned the gods of the ocean and that they were watching me.

I became aware of motion far overhead and glimpsed a great, amorphous blob the size of an unfurled sail, silhouetted against the dark water like a cloud in a night sky. The outer edge of its body rippled like a lady's lace shawl caught in the wind, and within its boneless body I saw an array of pulsing colors, going from golden orange to blood red to violet to blue and back again. Behind it trailed a forest of tendrils like a ragged bridal train, some as thin as a reed, while others were as thick as a strong man's arm.

As I watched the thing's progress, a green sea turtle swam into view. It was an impressive specimen, easily four feet long and two hundred pounds. Without warning, several of the tendrils snapped forth, wrapping themselves about the hapless creature while delivering numerous stings. The turtle struggled only briefly before going still, and the tendrils contracted, drawing it up into the gelatinous creature's body.

"Do not fear, cousin," Koro said reassuringly, although there was no way he could have spoken, nor I hear him, on the ocean floor. But such is the nature of dreams. "They will not harm you, for you carry the seal of the Naia." He pointed to the dolphin amulet I wore. "It grants you safe passage among all who share the blood of the Ocean Born."

"It didn't stop One-Eye and his clan from trying to kill me," I pointed out.

"One-Eye broke taboo," Koro replied solemnly. "And he and his tribe paid dearly for it; as will the *Absolom*, and all who sail on her."

I wanted to ask Koro what he meant, but before I could do so, there came the sound of whale song. It was louder than any I had ever heard through the hull of the ship, as if a choir of whale were celebrating High Mass. It was the most beautiful and eerie thing I had ever heard, in dreams or waking.

A mournful look passed over my friend's face. "Tangaroa's people are offering up their prayers for deliverance. The *Absolom* is doomed."

I awoke with a start, gasping like a man plucked from the sea. My forehead was damp with sweat and my heart beat against my ribs like as if knocking on a door. I automatically glanced toward Koro's bunk, and found the harpooner awake. He was looking back at me, still wearing the sad, worried expression I had seen in my dream.

Suddenly, from above decks I heard the look-out cry: "Thar she blows!"

Chapter Sixteen

The Harem Is Sighted—Koro Defiant—Koro And The Cat— The Truth Revealed—Back To The Sea

The dawn sky was red as blood as I emerged from below decks. There were already a number of hands crowding the starboard side, talking excitedly among themselves and pointing toward the horizon. Once I shouldered my way to the rail, I saw what had the crew in such a tizzy.

As far as the eye could see the ocean was full of whales, the great sea beasts dotting its surface like buffalo grazing on the prairie. Not only were there sperms to be had, but rights and humpbacks as well. I have never seen a pod of such size before, comprised of such different species.

"How many do you think there are?" Nicodemus asked in wonder.

"Easily a hundred, if not two," Cuppy replied. "I gave up countin' at twenty."

"Do you think its King Jim's harem?" This came from Pedro the cook. He was a thin fellow prone to nervousness and adhered to every superstition known to Man. About his neck, he wore a cross, the Jewish star, a rosary and any number of heathen symbols, all of which he constantly fingered during moments of anxiety.

"What else *could* it be?" Nicodemus snorted.

"What if King Jim attacks the ship?" Pedro asked, rattling his collection of icons. "What if he rams us like he did the *Virginia Dare*, seven years ago?"

"Then it will be the last thing the monster does."

Pedro, Cuppy, Nicodemus and I turned around, surprised to find Captain Godward standing behind us. He was staring out at the bounty spread before him, his eyes gleaming as they had when the fever was upon him.

"Where is Koro?" Godward asked, directing the question to me. "He's to serve as harpooner for Mr. Gussett."

Before I could reply, Koro emerged from the nearby gangway, his face as solemn as those that lined the shores of Easter Island. "I will not hunt these whales, Cap'n."

Godward recoiled as if the harpooner's words had been a blow. "How dare you speak to your betters in such a manner, boy?"

"I mean no disrespect, Captain," Koro replied. "But I refuse to break taboo. To kill these whales will bring the wrath of Tangaroa."

Godward's face turned as red as a boiled crab. "I don't care *what* your heathen religion forbids, you're on my ship, and I'm giving you an *order*, sailor! You are to report to Mr. Gussett immediately."

Koro shook his head, his mouth set into a resolute line. "What you would have me do is taboo. I can not be a part of it. I beg you, Captain —turn the ship around. The longer it stays here, the more sure its doom becomes."

This last part triggered an uneasy murmur among the assembled deckhands, which did not go unnoticed by the captain. "You dare disobey my direct order?" he bellowed. His eyes showed white all-around as if they were about to leap from his skull. "Whale Rider or not, I will take your hide for such insolence! Put that man in irons!" he commanded. A pair of able-bodies stepped forward and laid rough hands on Koro as a third came forth with a set of manacles. With a single flex of his powerful arms the islander escaped his would-be captors as if he was shrugging off a coat. One of them stumbled backward, landing at Godward's feet. "Get up, you dog!" The captain bellowed, delivering a swift kick to the seat of the fallen sailor's pants. He then turned to address the others. "Grab him, or I'll have the lot of you flogged as well!"

The threat of the cat was enough to spur the onlookers who had been hanging back into action. Koro struggled mightily as his shipmates grabbed at him, swinging his fists and feet as if they were cudgels, sending strong men flying in every direction. But Koro was but one man, and Captain Godward had an entire forecastle at his command, so it was not long before he was pinned down, three sailors to each limb. And yet still he writhed and bucked, like a landed tuna tossed on deck. As one of the hands bent down to try and clap a set of leg-irons about the islander's ankles, Koro lashed out a final time, catching the hapless sailor with his foot and breaking his jaw with a single blow.

"Never mind the irons!" Captain Godward snapped. "Just take him to the shrouds!"

The deckhands did as they were commanded, dragging the struggling Koro to the rigging that both kept the main mast from snapping off and provided a rope-ladder to the upper spar above. Although he fought them at every step, they still managed to seize him up and tie him to the shrouds. There was no need to strip the harpooner of his shirt as he never wore one. The intricate tattoos that covered his back jumped and rippled with the movement of his muscles as he tested the strength of his bonds.

Once he was sure the prisoner was secured and unable to escape, Captain Godward shouted: *"All hands witness punishment! Ahoy!"*

The cry was quickly taken up by Mulogo, and then echoed throughout the length and breadth of the ship. The various hands set aside their work to gather in the waist of the ship to watch the flogging. Even Hawley, still weak and feverish from his own beating, joined the throng. Satisfied that everyone from the cabin boy on up was in attendance, the captain turned to the Second Mate, who stood waiting at his elbow.

"Mr. Mulogo! Attend to the punishment!"

The smile on Mulogo's face as he took his place at the shrouds made my blood run cold. In place of the knotted rope he had used previously, the harpooner now carried a cat o'nine tails, the tips of which were barbed with bits of tin. Mulogo looked

Koro over like a butcher sizing up a side of beef, then snatched the pocket watch his rival wore about his neck, snapping the leather thong on which it hung as if it were a piece of string. Then, as an afterthought, he snatched the ever-present watch cap from the islander's head.

"No!" Koro cried, renewing his struggles to free himself with even greater determination.

The triumphant leer pasted across Mulogo's face dissolved instantly, to be replaced by a look of genuine horror. The African gave out a high-pitched, almost girlish shriek, and hurled the cap to the deck as if it was made of fire.

At first I could not understand what could possibly provoke such a show of terror from such a hardened sailor as Mulogo. Then I looked at Koro's head, now exposed for the first time since we met, and the blow-hole at the top of his skull. The first thing I noticed was that the islander was completely bald; the second was the blow-hole at the top of his skull. As I stared, dumbstruck, the muscular flap of the blowhole abruptly dilated and made the clicking-whistle familiar to all mariners. The assembled crew gasped in alarm and more than a few crossed themselves.

"He's one of those monsters!" Cuppy shouted, made angry by his fear. "Like the ones that killed Cap'n Solomon!"

"Kill the bastard!" Pedro the Cook screamed, waving his meat-cleaver for emphasis. "Gut him like a fish!"

The rest of the crew yelled in agreement, brandishing knives, belaying pins and boat-hooks like angry soldiers preparing to storm a castle. Within a heartbeat, they had forgotten the countless times they had sung Koro's praises as a harpooner, all the meals they had shared with him, and how it was he who had slain the creature who had murdered their beloved Captain Solomon. What had been their shipmate mere moments before was now a fiend from hell, no different in their eyes than a kraken, sea serpent, or any other monster that haunted the uncharted depths of the ocean.

With an inhuman squeal, Koro tore himself free of the shrouds like a dolphin breaking free of a fisherman's net, and made a mad dash for the gunwale.

"Stop the prisoner!" Captain Godward hollered. "Don't let him get away!"

One of the hands from the fo'c'sle moved to block Koro's escape, but the harpooner barreled into him, sending him flying like a sack of grain. With a single bound, he leapt half the breadth of the deck, landing atop the gunwale as the angry crew surged forward, howling for his blood. Without a single glance back, my only friend in the world dove head-first into the waiting sea as his former shipmates charged the rail, baying like a pack hounds after a fox.

Part Six
The Eye of Tangaroa

Chapter Seventeen

The Tattooed Dolphin—I, Jonah—A Moment's Reprieve—I Am Exiled

Without a moment's hesitation, Koro leapt from the *Absolom* and plunged headlong into the ocean, which closed about him with nary a ripple to mark his passing. The outraged crew crowded the rail, hurling everything from curses to harpoons after him.

A few moments later a dolphin abruptly leapt forth from the waves off the port bow, its skin gleaming like polished stone. As it somersaulted in mid-air, it revealed an intricate tattoo on its under-belly before splashing back down and disappearing for good.

"The devil mocks us!" Mulogo shouted angrily. My bowels turned to water as he turned and jabbed his finger in my direction. "Padgett is the one who brought the monster aboard in the first place! *He* is the one who brought evil among us!"

The crew of the *Absolom* turned as one to scowl at me. Although I had worked, eaten, slept and shat alongside them for two years, at that moment they were worse than strangers to me.

"Aye, thicker than thieves they were," Cuppy agreed, nodding his snowy head, "always keeping one another's company, like a warlock and his familiar."

"Yes, Koro was my friend; I don't deny that!" I replied, trying desperately to make myself heard over the collected grumbling of the crew. "But you *must* believe I did *not* know he wasn't human!" Of course, that was last part was not exactly true, and the others could hear the nervousness in my voice.

"The man's a wizard!" Mulogo shouted, drowning out my denials. "He controls the creature with that amulet he always wears! That is why he is never without it!"

"It is a bequest from my uncle, nothing more!" I protested, my hand instinctively closing about the pendant. And then, in my eagerness to clear myself of suspicion, I carelessly blurted out: *"I am no wizard, this I swear, or my name isn't Jonah Padgett!"*

As I heard myself speak, my heart tumbled from its perch, but there was nothing I could to do to make it right. There is no calling back words once they are spoken—especially those said in front of so many witnesses.

Mr. Gusset stepped forward, eyeing me like a rabid rat he'd flushed from the bilge. *"What* did you say your name was, boy?"

"J-Jonas," I stammered, doing my best to sound truthful.

The First Mate grimaced at my lie as if he'd bit into a lemon. "This man's a Jonah in both deed *and* name!"

There was a ragged roar of anger, as if every hand aboard the *Absolom* had one throat, and the crew abruptly surged forward. I found myself buffeted about in a human maelstrom, subjected to kicks, punches, and slaps from all sides, before finally being grabbed by a half-hundred hands and lifted bodily from the deck.

"Throw the Jonah overboard!" Mulogo bellowed. *"Toss him to the sharks!"*

And they would have done it, too, without a moment's thought or remorse, had there not come the explosive report of a gun. The rabble fell instantly silent as Captain Godward waded through their number, a smoking Navy Colt clutched in one hand, kicking aside those who moved too slowly for his liking.

"Set that man down!" he barked.

My attackers immediately did as commanded, and I heaved a sigh of relief as my boots once more touched the deck.

"We may be on the open seas, but this ship flies under an American flag!" The skipper said, his voice raised loud enough for all to hear. "And I'll not stand by and watch a fellow countryman murdered in cold blood, warlock or not!"

"Bless you, Cap'n," I said gratefully.

"Don't go thanking me just *yet*, Mr. Padgett," he snarled, eyeing me as he would a maggot crawling about in his breakfast bacon. "The truth of the matter is the men will mutiny if I allow you to remain onboard. So I have decided to place you in my gig, along with some provisions, and tether you to the stern of the ship. Once we are done in these waters, I will see to it that you are put ashore at Rapa Nui."

"You're going to leave me in an open boat for a fortnight, maybe more?" I exclaimed. "You might as well put a bullet between my eyes!"

"Do not tempt me, Mr. Padgett," he replied darkly.

Despite his obvious distaste for me, Godward was true to his word and converted the boat that normally served as the captain's private taxi while in harbor into my floating prison. The dinghy was smaller and lighter than the whaleboats, but nowhere near as sea-worthy, and was outfitted with a can of sea biscuits and a cask of water. After removing the oars, Mulogo tied one end of a lengthy coil of rope to the bow-line of the captain's gig, the other end of which was secured to the stern of the *Absolom*, then ordered it lowered over the side. I was then forced, at pistol-point, to climb down a rope ladder to the waiting boat, which pitched and wallowed sharply in the chop of the ocean. The moment I dropped into the dinghy, the ladder was immediately pulled up and Mulogo hurled my sea bag after me.

As dangerous as being in an open boat on the high seas might be, by that point I was eager to escape the *Absolom*. I had noticed more than one crewman eyeing me while fingering their knives, and it was only a matter of time before one of them slipped a blade between my ribs, captain's orders or not.

And so the *Absolom* continued on its course, sailing headlong into King Jim's harem, all the while towing me along like a recalcitrant hound brought to heel.

Chapter Eighteen

In Absolom's Wake—The Hunters Return—A Cradle Rocked By Sharks—A Dream of Gusset—The Blood-Red Dawn

Exiled to *Absolom's* wake, I could do nothing but sit in my open-air prison and watch as Captain Godward and his officers lowered their whaleboats and set out to raid King Jim's harem. Once they finally dwindled from view, I set about making myself as comfortable as possible in my new surroundings.

The sun, at such latitudes, is brutal, and I knew I was in far greater danger of dying of heatstroke than a shark's bite. So I busied myself by tying together what few articles of clothing were in my sea bag and stretching them between the gunwales at the bow, in hopes of creating both shelter and shade. As the sun was extremely hot, it wasn't long before I was completely drenched in sweat and burning with thirst. I inspected the small barrel of water given me, which held nine gallons of fresh water. While that might sound like more than enough water for a single man, it does not take into account the constant broiling sun which, even on board ship, will parch a sailor's tongue until it feels like sand paper, or the fact I was looking at a fortnight or more exposed to the elements. It would take superhuman willpower, and far better luck than I had been enjoying of late, to survive more than a week under such circumstances.

I opened the spigot on the barrel and decanted some of the precious fluid into a battered tin cup. Although the water was stale and warm, I had to fight the urge to fill my cup a second time.

Hours later, just as the sun began its descent, I heard the

unmistakable sound of oarsmen singing off in the distance. I squinted in the direction of the voices and saw one of the whaleboats returning with a dead sperm whale in tow. I was not surprised to see that it was Mulogo's boat that had claimed the first kill, for now that Koro was gone, he reigned supreme as the *Absolom's* finest hunter.

I watched from afar as my former shipmates set about the cutting-in, turning the sea red with the blood from the dead whale. As the crimson continued to spread, sharks rose from the briny deep like housewives hurrying to the butcher shop.

By the time the sun had all but slipped from the sky, Captain Godward's boat arrived with its catch—this time a right whale. Since the first kill was still in the process of being butchered, the second whale had to be tethered at the ship's prow to await its turn.

For the rest of the night the *Absolom* burned like a barque from Hell, its masts lit by the fires of the try-works as gouts of foul, greasy black smoke rose into the sky. Even in exile, there was no escaping the stink of boiling blubber. I sat there in the flickering darkness, bobbing about on the end of several hundred yards of rope like the cork on a fishing line, listening to my former shipmates shout, curse and sing as they labored to fill the cargo hold. Never, in all my months at sea, did I pine for my childhood home as I did that night for my cooper's bench and narrow bunk. Indeed, the noisome confines of the foc'sle now seemed as welcome as my mother's embrace.

Although the sun had finally disappeared, night brought little relief, as all it did was replace the broiling heat of the day with a stifling humidity that lay against my skin like a towel in a Turkish bath. It wasn't until I finished consuming a humble repast of hardtack soaked in water that it occurred to me that the third whaleboat—the one piloted by Mr. Gusset—had yet to return. Finding one's way back to the ship in the dark can be extremely difficult, but at least the fires from the try-works could be seen for miles, effectively turning the *Absolom* into a beacon for its errant children. Indeed, there was enough light that I could easily make out the figure of Captain Godward atop the poop deck, awaiting the return of his First Mate.

Having fed myself, I folded my emptied sea-bag into a makeshift pillow and settled down in the bottom of the boat, my head to the bow, and my feet toward the stern. With its high gunwales and the unceasing movement of the waves and the occasional thump from a passing shark, it was not unlike being rocked in a cradle and I soon fell asleep.

I dreamt I saw Koro treading water not far from my boat, bobbing up and down like a buoy. Although he did speak to me, I knew he wanted to show me something and I leapt from the boat without a moment's hesitation. The moment I entered the water, Koro disappeared and in his place was a dolphin with skin that gleamed like a polished stone. I grabbed its dorsal fin and it towed me though the water at breakneck speed.

When the dolphin finally halted, I found myself staring at the flotsam of what had once been the whaleboat piloted by Mr. Gusset. The bo'sun-turned-first mate was still clinging to the wreckage with the last of his strength. I scanned the surrounding water, but there was not a trace of the other men. With an agonized groan, Gusset surrendered his hold and slid beneath the waves, joining his shipmates in Davy Jones' locker. The moment he sank beneath the surface, there came a dreadful great sound, like the bellow of an animal, but in a register so low it vibrated the marrow in my bones. But as I turned to ask Koro what might possibly give voice to such a frightful call, I found that I was alone, and I knew, with the certainty of knowledge that comes with dreams, that whatever had voiced that fearsome challenge was headed my way...

I awoke with a start and sat bolt upright, my heart hammering away like a blacksmith at his forge. The night was no more, and in its place was a dawn that dyed the early morning sky the same shade of red as the whale's blood staining the water that surrounded me.

Chapter Nineteen

The Collision—The Wrath of King Jim—The Fate of the Absolom—The Eye of Tangaroa

Shortly after dawn, Captain Godward resumed his watch atop the poopdeck. His manner was noticeably agitated, even from my distant vantage point. As he searched with his spyglass for sign of Gusset and the others, I remembered what Koro had shown me in my dream and knew with dreadful certainty that the missing whaleboat would never return. The day continued to progress, and as the sun crossed the yard-arm I heard the look-out in the crow's nest shout: *"Thar she blows! Off the starboard bow!"*

There, in the near distance, sat a bull sperm whale so large that if I had not seen its flukes, I would have mistaken it for a small, barren island thrust up from the ocean floor. The beast's skin was black as a bible and the plume that shot from its spout was taller than a church steeple. There was no mistaking this whale for any other—we were in the presence of his royal highness, King Jim.

Captain Godward began shouting at the crew, yelling at them to ready the boats for the greatest hunt of their lives. Just then, as the deck hands scrambled to launch the whaleboats, a man's hand emerged from the water just beyond the bow of my boat. The hand was webbed and clutched a blade fashioned from obsidian, which it used to slice through the rope tethering the dinghy to the stern of the ship.

"Koro!" I exclaimed, and then quickly clamped a hand over

my mouth, for fear of attracting attention. A few moments later, the remaining length of rope that was attached to the bow-line went taut, like the line on a fishing pole that's hooked a fish, and the dinghy reversed itself and began to move in the opposite direction of the ship. Suddenly there came the sound of the alarm-bell, and I assumed one of the deckhands had noticed my getaway.

I turned around, fearing that I might still be within rifle-shot of the *Absolom,* and was astounded to see King Jim rapidly propelling himself toward the ship by churning the ocean with his massive flukes. In all my months at sea, I had never seen a whale charge a ship before. But then, King Jim was no ordinary whale, but a ship-killer, made famous when he attacked the *Virginia Dare,* a decade before. As the crew of the Absalom ran frantically to and fro, Captain Godward snatched up his harpoon and dashed forward in hopes of spearing the monster from the deck of the ship—only to have King Jim plow into the starboard side, just short of the prow.

There came the terrible sound of snapping timbers, followed by horrified screams as those hands still in the rigging were sent flying from their perches. Some of them landed with bone-splintering force onto the decks below, while others were catapulted into the shark-infested water. As for King Jim, the impact barely slowed him down as he passed under the ship, causing the *Absolom* to rock violently from side to side.

A few seconds later the great whale surfaced close on the port side, where he lay, apparently stunned, with his head by the bow and his tail toward the stern. Both Captain Godward and Mulogo hurried forward with their harpoons, looping the ropes attached to them about a nearby capstan. But upon realizing the leviathan's tail was too close to the ship, Mulogo lowered his weapon. Captain Godward, however, was so given over to the hunt he launched his harpoon at the monster whale's vast heart.

The moment the barbed lance sank into his ink-black hide, King Jim snapped back to wakefulness and with a single slap of his mighty tail reduced the *Absolom's* rudder to kindling before sounding. As the league of rope played out, the capstan began to spin like a top and the ship listed dangerously to port, causing everything not nailed down to tumble across the deck, including the huge cast-iron kettles set atop the try-works. A chorus of agonized screams rang out as hapless sailors found themselves doused in boiling oil and crushed against the bulwarks. Then, to add to the horror, the door to one of the brick furnaces flew open, spilling forth fire.

Captain Godward quickly rallied his remaining crew, ordering them to man the bilge pumps in hopes of extinguishing the fire before it reached the sails above or the oil-laden cargo hold below. And for a brief moment it looked like they would succeed—and then King Jim returned. But this time he was no longer a whale, but a thing born of myths and nightmares.

From the waist up he was shaped like a man, in that there was a head, torso and two limbs, but after that the resemblance ended. The head was massive, with a bulbous brow that thrust forward like the bow of a ship, and was joined to a pair of shoulders as wide as a redwood by a short, thickly muscled neck. The eyes were set way back and far apart, and what I can only call his 'face' lacked nose, cheekbones, lips, or hair of any kind.

King Jim opened his long, narrow lower jaw, exposing peg-like teeth the size of a man's fist and issued forth the dreadful bellow I had heard in my dream. The sound of his royal displeasure was enough to make me clap my hands over my ears. He then tore free the carcasses of the slaughtered whales tethered to the Absalom, snapping the ropes and chains of the blocks and tackles as if they were made of twine.

Captain Godward, Mulogo and what men were now left, all carrying rifles from the armory, rushed to the bulwarks and opened fire on the leviathan. The volley of lead seemed to do little to King Jim, save anger him further. With a second ear-splitting bellow, the behemoth snatched up the captain and his mate as if they were dolls and crushed the life out of them. Even though he was always a devil to me, I will carry the sound of Mulogo's death scream to my grave.

King Jim then grabbed the foremast and wrenched it from its moorings, like a barber-surgeon yanking out a recalcitrant tooth, and used it to bludgeon the ship, sending the terrified deckhands fleeing in all directions. Once the mast was reduced to kindling, the monster brought a massive fist down onto the burning foredeck, like a spoiled child taking out his temper on his toys. Already weakened by the collision, the hull gave way with an explosive groan and began taking on water. As the ship sank, King Jim continued his assault by snapping the mainmast in half and using it like a harpoon to punch further holes in the body of the ship. Within minutes the *Absolom* was reduced to nothing more than splinters and torn sailcloth, taking all aboard to the depths below.

As the broken masts sank out of sight, I wept like an orphaned child before his mother's grave. For two years the Absalom had been my only home, and its crew the only people I knew. And although they crew had turned against me, they did not deserve such a cruel and monstrous fate.

However, my grief for my shipmates was quickly replaced by mortal terror as King Jim swung about his monstrous head and saw the lonesome captain's gig bobbing atop the waves. The fearsome creature closed the distance between us with a single swish of his powerful tail, barreling towards me like a living juggernaut. I cried out in horror and instinctively raised my arms in a vain attempt to block the sight of the monster's upraised fist. But, to my surprise, the blow never fell.

It took all my courage, but I finally lowered my hands and saw King Jim towering over me like a living mountain, his breath hissing and rumbling from the blowhole atop his head like a steam locomotive standing at the station. Although it is foolish to ascribe human emotions to something so inhuman, there seemed to be a look of confusion on what passed for his face.

Without warning, King Jim gave voice to yet another of his fearsome roars and scooped up the captain's gig in one vast hand. As I clung to the gunwales for dear life, the sight of his gaping maw made me fear I would end up in the belly of a whale, just like my biblical namesake. But, to my surprise, I was not devoured. Instead, the giant carefully brought the uplifted boat closer to what I can only call his face, like a near-sighted man inspecting the detail on a model ship.

Although King Jim's eyes were the size of grapefruit, they were tiny in comparison to the rest of his massive bulk. As terrified as I was, I could not bring myself to look away as he studied me, and I glimpsed in their depths a vast intellect, born before the islands rose from the ocean floor. Suddenly, I knew what it was that had caught his attention. With trembling hands, I removed the dolphin amulet from about my neck and held it up. And I saw the flicker of confusion in the giant eye turn into a gleam of recognition. King Jim then gently returned my boat to the water and gave it a small push, like a boy playing admiral in a pond, which sent it shooting forward as if under full sail.

His wrath exhausted and his brides avenged, King Jim— better known as Tangaroa, Lord of the Ocean— rose up on his tail and, with an oddly graceful pirouette for a being his size, dropped into the water with a thunderous splash.

Chapter Twenty

Beyond Reason—I Am Adrift—A Gift From Below—The Ship Beneath The Waves—A Savage Savior

As King Jim returned to the crushing depths of his kingdom, my nerves, already stretched to their breaking point, snapped altogether. I collapsed in a heap as I alternated between screams of laughter and gut-wrenching sobs. There is no shame in admitting I succumbed to madness after all I had endured, and anyone who claims they could have kept their sanity intact under such circumstances is a damn liar.

I do not remember much of what occurred while I was beyond reason save that I traveled so far into madness I eventually came out the other side. In fact, I daresay I emerged far saner than I ever was before— although there are many who would argue this point. My sense of time was lost along with my mind, and I have no true idea how long I remained in such a state: it could have been hours, it might have been days. All I know is that when I came back to my senses, I was lying flat on my back at the bottom of the boat, staring up a sky filled with pin-wheeling stars and my mouth was so dry I couldn't spit into a thimble.

I crawled over to the water cask and slaked my thirst as much as I dared. I then became aware that I was horribly sunburned from scalp to toe. My skin radiated heat like a stove-top, and every movement of my body brought sharp, stinging pain, as if beset by angry hornets. My discomfort was such that it was impossible for me to sleep, despite my exhaustion.

At length the morning came and the sun rose on a world

made of water, without a sail in sight. The fact I saw no wreckage from the *Absolom*—not even the tiniest of splinters—told me I had been at sea, both physically and mentally, for at least a day, possibly more. The dawn also brought the realization that my supply of water was dangerously low and that I was down to two sea biscuits.

As the sun continued its inexorable climb, I did what I could to protect my scorched flesh from its merciless rays. Large swathes of peeling skin hung from my shoulders and arms like cobwebs, but there was only so much shade to be found in my floating prison. I spent most of the day scanning the horizon in hopes of spotting a sail, but all I could see was sky and water, each as blue as the other. At times I felt as if I was suspended between the two elements and in danger at any moment of drifting off through the clouds.

I not only searched for passing ships, but also sought the ever-shifting sea for some glimpse of Koro. But I had yet to see any evidence of him since the destruction of the *Absolom*. Once I thought I saw a flash of dolphin fin, but it was only a reef shark chasing a school of fish. II was truly on my own, with nothing but my wits and will to keep me alive.

I did not eat until after dark, as the heat of the day robbed me of any appetite. Even then, I had a hard time keeping down what little food left to me, as my body was wracked with fever and chills. Eventually I drifted into a fitful sleep, curled up in the bow of the boat. As miserable as it was, that first day out of madness became the template for my life as a castaway.

Each day the sun scorched me to the bone, and each day I spent the daylight hours parched with thirst. I had no choice but to parcel out what little water was left, granting myself only three swallows a day. The food ran out well before the water, of course, and two days after my final meal, my belly began tying itself into painful knots. My hunger even followed me into my dreams, taunting me with visions of suckling pigs roasting on a spit, wheels of cheese and loaves of fresh-baked bread.

Two days after that, the water in the cask began to take on a brackish taste, and I knew it would not be long before it would go the way of the food. But what concerned me even more was the fact my strength was rapidly eroding. My body was beginning to cannibalize itself, and soon I would no longer be able to keep watch for ships or signal should one pass by.

Then, on the fifth day, I was jarred from my fitful sleep by something wet slapping against my blistered flesh. I instinctively shouted and flailed about in alarm, causing the dinghy to rock dangerously back and forth. Once I could focus my eyes, I discovered a mackerel lying beside me. At first I thought it had jumped into the boat, as fish are sometimes wont to do. Then I realized that not only was the mackerel quite dead, it had been sliced open from gills to tail and neatly disemboweled.

A burst of excitement shot through my exhausted body, spurring me to raise myself up on my knees and gaze about. "*Koro!*" I called out, my voice hoarse from thirst. "Koro, my brother! Where are you?" As much as I longed for an answer, the surface of the ocean remained still and smooth as glass. Once I realized there would be no response, I turned my attention to the fish and greedily fed upon its raw, moist flesh. When I finished my feast, I lay back down, secure in the knowledge that while I might still be the sole survivor of the *Absolom*, I was no longer alone.

The next day, I saw, or thought I saw, a vessel. It was dusk, and my eye was caught by a glow on the near horizon. As I struggled upright onto the bench at the stern of the boat, I spotted a sailing ship with three masts with five sails each plowing across the ocean in my direction! As it came closer I could hear music being played and voices being raised in song and laughter. I tore my makeshift tent from where it was stretched across the bow and frantically waved it above my head with the last of my strength.

"*Ahoy!*" I croaked. "*Ship ahoy!*"

But as what I hoped was my salvation drew nearer, it occurred to me that the light aboard the ship did not come from lanterns but radiated from the vessel itself. I remembered old Cuppy's story about the *Caleuche*, and quickly fell silent. As I did so, the ghost-ship disappeared beneath waves, where it glowed like the moon reflected in the ocean surf. As it continued to sail underwater I saw figures moving about on the deck, some of whom were familiar to me. I could see Cuppy, Hawley, and Gusset, even Mr. Shreve, Mulogo and Captain Godward, laughing and dancing the hornpipe, as if they no longer had a care in the world. And standing on the poop deck, overlooking the festivities, was none other than Captain Solomon, and on his arm was a beautiful woman with blonde hair that floated about her head like a cloud and whose body was half-covered in golden scales.

The next day I drank the last swallow of water. As the sun poured its heat onto me, I was convinced my final hour was at hand. My vision had been steadily fading ever since I had seen the ghost-ship and although it was high noon, I couldn't see beyond my outstretched hand.

At some point I must have drifted into unconsciousness, for I was suddenly jarred awake by the sound of human voices. Thinking the *Caleuche* had returned to claim me for its crew, I managed to raise myself up again and saw a whaleboat headed in my direction. Standing in the bow was a towering Maori covered in tattoos and holding a harpoon. He smiled reassuringly as he reached out for me, revealing a mouth full of teeth that had been filed to a point. While such a savage visage would have struck horror into the hearts of most, I would have wept at its beauty had the sun not already burned the tears from my eyes.

Epilog

As luck would have it, the ship responsible for plucking me from my floating tomb was none other than *The Pilgrimage*, back hunting whales after replenishing her crew in Chile.I was full of fever and nothing else when the Maori pulled me into his boat, and it speaks to the Christian charity of Captain Fastnacht that he brought me into his own quarters and personally saw to it that I was nursed back to health.

While delirious I babbled about whale-gods, dolphin-princes and princesses, shark-men, drowned cities and ghost-ships, but, given my condition, no one seemed to pay them much heed. Or perhaps, having experienced King Jim's wrath, Captain Fastnacht knew more than he was willing to admit. In any case, once my fever broke, I made sure to say nothing more, and never explained how it was I ended up in the captain's gig in the first place. The last thing I wanted was to once more be branded a Jonah and thrown back into the sea.

I spent the next four months aboard the *Pilgrimage*, working as I had upon the *Absolom* to earn my keep. When the ship dropped anchor in Tahiti, I bid my farewell to Captain Fastnacht, who I had grown quite fond of. I never saw him, or the *Pilgrimage*, ever again. As it turned out, I had arrived in Papeete at a most fortuitous time. The Franco-Tahitian War had just ended, and I was hired by a Mr. William Stewart to help oversee a thousand Chinese brought in to work on his vast cotton plantation. After five years, I had saved up enough money to do as I liked. So I quit my job and booked passage to the Sandwich Islands, as they were still called back then.

A dozen years ago I bought a parcel of land on the island of

Hawaii near the ocean and built a house for myself in the native style. My wants are simple and my needs few. In many ways, I have taken His Lordship, who died so bravely on the shores of his adopted land, as my role model. I dine on what I pull from the sea in my nets or what I pluck from the fruiting trees that grow on my land. When I weary of the native palm wine, I go to the nearest white settlement and barter for rum.

Although I keep to myself, my brush with the fabled ship-killer, King Jim, and status as the sole survivor of the *Absolom* have made me something of a local "character", as they say. Over the years, numerous visitors have found their way to my hut, gifting me with bottles of whisky and tinned meat in exchange for my story. The Europeans, as well as my fellow Yankees, here on the Big Island argue amongst themselves as to whether I am a hermit or a beachcomber, but all agree that I am a drunkard and a sorry excuse for a white man. As for the Islanders, they view me differently. To them I am a *kahuna*—a shaman, of sorts—one touched by the gods of the ocean, as evidenced by the dolphin amulet I still wear about my neck. They give me offerings of food and palm wine to bless their fishing nets and outriggers, and on occasion send me their daughters to keep me company.

It has been twenty years since I left my family to go a'whalin'. I am certain my mother and father are no more, and what siblings remain would find me more stranger than brother, should I return. Besides, I have heard disturbing stories of a war amongst the states; why should I leave paradise for such a Hell? And it's not as if I don't have family in this part of the world as well.

Not long ago a young man came to visit me. He carried with him a newspaper that claimed that King Jim had been hunted down and killed the year before. There was even an engraving of the dead whale placed on a scale, which held in its balance several elephants, to better illustrate its immensity. When he asked me what I thought of the report, I laughed at the very idea of King Jim being boiled down and used to light a parlor in Baltimore. I told him that what they had caught was one of his many sons, but not the king himself. The young man was clearly unconvinced by my claims, and I realized that the spoken word of someone with first-hand knowledge was nowhere as real to him as the written word of someone half a world away.

So that is why I am putting the story—the *true* story—of what befell the *Absolom* on paper. However, I do not plan to see it published any time soon, as I am in no great hurry to have myself declared mad. While I may no longer have to fear being called a Jonah and stranded at sea, being clapped up in a lunatic asylum is another matter altogether. No, once I have finished my narrative, I will deliver it to my solicitor in Hilo, with the directive that it not be read, or published, until I have died—or assumed dead.

No doubt, if you have followed my story thus far, kind reader, you are asking yourself: 'But what became of Koro? Did you ever see him again?'

The answer to your question is both yes and no. While I have not clapped eyes on him since the day he cut me free of the *Absolom*, he often comes to me in dreams. Sometimes he is in the form of a dolphin, but most often he appears to me as a man. In my dreams he shows me things, such as how to bring the fish closer to shore, protect against the sharks, and calm the storms, as any good *kahuna* should. And I know, as sure as the sun is hot and water wet, my kinsman will one day soon rise from the waves beyond my door to escort me into the sunken city of the Ocean Born.

And so I leave you now, whoever you might be, to read my words and judge for yourself as to whether I am truthful, mad or a liar.

But I warn you: I am all three.

About the Author

Nancy A. Collins is the award-winning author of numerous weird and creepy stories, but she is perhaps best known for the punk vampire slayer Sonja Blue. She is also credited as a founder of the urban fantasy genre. She is the only woman to have written *Swamp Thing* for DC Comics, and the first woman to have served as a writer for *Vampirella*. Her most recent works are the three-volume *Golgotham* series and the *Army of Darkness: Furious Road* miniseries for Dynamite Comics. She currently resides in the Atlanta Metro Area.

Curious about other Crossroad Press books?
Stop by our site:
http://store.crossroadpress.com
We offer quality writing
in digital, audio, and print formats.

Enter the code FIRSTBOOK
to get 20% off your first order from our store!
Stop by today!